BOOK
3

the NEW
sugar
creek gang

The Case of the
Cold Turkey

Pauline Hutchens Wilson
Sandy Dengler

D0638922

MOODY PRESS
CHICAGO

© 2001 by
PAULINE HUTCHENS WILSON

Library of Congress Cataloging-in-Publication Data

Wilson, Pauline Hutchens.
    The case of the cold turkey / Pauline Hutchens
Wilson and Sandy Dengler.
      p. cm. – (New Sugar Creek Gang ; 3)
    Summary: When the shelter where he and Tiny
volunteer fills up with injured fawns and rabbits,
eleven-year-old Les and his friends in the New
Sugar Creek Gang try to discover what kind of
wild animals are attacking them.
    ISBN 0-8024-8663-0
    [1. Animal rescue–Fiction. 2. Feral animals–Fiction.
3. Christian life–Fiction. 4. Mystery and detective
stories.] I. Dengler, Sandy. II. Title.

PZ7.W69758 Cam 2001
[Fic]–dc21

                                            00-065392

                    1 3 5 7 9 10 8 6 4 2

        Printed in the United States of America

INTRODUCTION

"It just isn't the same."

My dad sounded so sad. We stood on the walk-way of a freeway overpass, looking out across a sea of new houses. Miles of houses, street after street.

"That line of trees out there is Sugar Creek." He waved an arm toward the hives of condos. "All this used to be farmland. When Paul Hutchens wrote those books about the Sugar Creek Gang, this is the area he wrote about. Right here."

I'm eleven, and, according to Dad, I'm older than most of the *homes* out here. "At least there's still a Sugar Creek," I said. "How far is it from our new place?"

"Couple miles. But the past—that was another world." He looked at me. "I'm sorry the fun is gone."

Dad walked down the slope to our car. I fell in behind him, wishing he didn't feel so sad.

When I was little, he read to me every night. And my favorite books to read were about a bunch of kids called the Sugar Creek Gang. They lived on farms near a creek and had a zil-lion adventures, mostly out in nature somewhere.

When Dad switched jobs, he found out we were going to move into the very area where the stories took place. He got all excited. I think he expected to find those farms here yet.

He grew up on a farm, so he knows a lot about that stuff. Every few pages, Dad would stop reading and say, "Now, Les, let me tell you about—" and then he'd explain something about spiders or shitepokes or whatever the story was talking about. So good old Les—that's me—learned a lot about farm life and nature when I was little, even though we lived in town.

We drove back to our brand-new home. It was an older house on a shady little back street. Just then it was full of boxes that the moving van had dumped the day before. And I mean full. Not very homey yet, but our beds were put together and made up, so who needs more?

Early next morning, I put on my jacket and found my helmet. It took me a while to dig my bike out of the garageful of jumbled stuff. Then I rode off, heading west.

So Dad thought the fun was gone. I wasn't so sure. That broad strip of trees along the creek looked awfully inviting.

I figured maybe I could find something interesting there. So that's how it all started.

I never guessed that I'd get all wrapped up in a real, true adventure like the ones we'd read about. And I would never *ever* have guessed that the Sugar Creek Gang would come back.

PAULINE HUTCHENS WILSON

1

As I look back, I guess it all started when our grocery store over in the strip mall put fresh turkeys on sale for half price. If they hadn't done that, I wouldn't have made a major career decision. And the new Sugar Creek Gang would not have gotten tangled up in a wolf scare. Well, on second thought, maybe we would have anyway. We tend to do that—get mixed up in stuff, I mean.

There are five of us, as weirdly different as you could imagine. I, Les Walker, am redheaded and freckled and never tan. Burn, yes. Tan, no. Bits, who lives across the street (her name is really Elizabeth Ware), tans just fine. She has plain brown hair in a ponytail.

Mike Alvarado and Tiny (Clarence Wilson on his school records) live close to each other. Tiny is extra tall and extra thin for his age, and Mike is stocky like his dad and short for his age, which is ten, a year younger than the rest of us. Tiny's black skin doesn't mind sun a bit. Neither does Mike's brownish one. Mike claims he has some Yaqui blood in him, but his blood looks just like mine when he cuts himself.

And then there's Lynn Wing, with her Chinese dad and Japanese mom. Except, she insists, her parents really aren't Chinese and

Japanese. They're American, as their parents were before them. But the family way back was Asian. She is quiet and slight, and you don't notice her. But when you need bright ideas in a hurry, she has them.

The thing that ties us together is Sugar Creek. We all five enjoy the old Sugar Creek Gang adventure books. That's what brought us together in the first place. Best of all, we live within a couple miles of the real Sugar Creek, which is now in a county park. We go there all the time.

Anyway, let me tell you about the wolf scare. And that turkey.

* * *

There is shopping, and there is shopping. My mom takes me shopping mostly so I can carry stuff. My sisters, Catherine and Hannah, are older than I, and they love it. I am bored out of my skull five minutes into the trip—like before the car even gets to the mall.

Except when it's groceries we're shopping for. Now that's different. I enjoy shopping in the grocery store. Mom chooses practical stuff, reads labels, and shops for value. I tend to shop for shape. For example, asparagus and green beans are not a good shape. Potato chips and tortilla chips are.

We were in the meat section that fateful day. The huge, long cold cases displayed the packaged meats. Mom leans strongly toward chicken, and she does wonderful things with it. She doesn't buy parts. She buys the whole corpse and cuts it up herself.

And here, in one of those big bins that's shaped like a chest freezer, was the "Special." Fresh turkeys. My first thought was, *Why turkey? It's not Thanksgiving.* But then I got to thinking about the warm, happy taste of turkey, a delight that should not be limited to one day in three hundred sixty- five.

I called, "Hey, Mom? You love bargains. Look here."

Hannah, fourteen, sniffed. "Why turkey? It's not Thanksgiving." Hannah was very quick to point out that good ideas never *ever* come from little brothers.

Mom looked in the bin. "Good price." She shoved a few aside to look at others. "Les? Which would you pick as best?"

I know a trick question when I hear it. "Well, if these were chickens, I'd say pick the heaviest. A batch of chickens are all about the same age, and the heavier ones have more meat per bone. But I don't know if that applies to turkeys. Does it?"

She shrugged. "I have no idea. I was hoping you knew." But the way she smiled, I knew it had been a test and that I'd answered right.

Mom picked a big one with a lot of yellow in the skin. I bucked it up into her cart for her.

Pushing the cart, I followed her down the next aisle. "Mom? Do they ever make turkey l'orange like they do duck? How about turkey au vin? That kind of thing. All I've ever seen a turkey is roasted."

"Come to think of it—" she pursed her lips, "—I have many recipes for turkey, but they all start with cooked leftovers."

"There's gotta be more than roasting." I pondered this question as I mindlessly shoved the cart along behind her.

Next, I thought: *Most chefs are men. They don't just instantly become great chefs; they must spend years practicing. But some are fairly young. Therefore they were cooking at my age, probably— eleven or so. No time to start like the present.*

"Mom? Chefs make a lot of money, don't they?"

"The good ones do. Yes."

"If I were a chef, I'd be the best."

I tried to imagine how neat it would be to be able to just bomb around in the kitchen awhile and whip up some fantastic dish. "Mom? Can I cook the turkey? Please?"

She stared at nothing for a moment. "Sure." *Yee ha!*

Catherine, the sister who's a year older than I, met us at midaisle with her load of cereal. We take turns picking out cereals, and this was her day. She dumped them in the basket. "Why turkey? It's not Thanksgiving."

Mom smiled. "It's for your brother to practice on. He's going to become a great chef."

2

As I walked in the door of the animal rescue shelter, tall, gangly Tiny yelled, "Man, Les, am I glad to see you! Gimme a hand here!"

You know, a greeting like that makes a body feel real good. It's almost always nice to know you're needed. I say *almost* because occasionally I'm needed to wash dishes. That's not so nice.

But Tiny really did need me today. Cages of various sizes lined one wall of the long, windowless reception room, and nearly all of them held injured wild animals. The food dishes hadn't been taken care of yet, the gurneys and examination tables were dirty and blood-streaked, the floor was a mess, and . . .

At the big exam table by the door, Tiny and a gray-haired woman in blue jeans tussled with a struggling fawn. The front of the lady's clothes were all smeared with blood—the fawn's blood, obviously. She must have carried it in the way you carry a small dog, pressed close to her.

Tiny had tied the little guy's legs together, but it still managed to throw itself around. The woman held it as best she could. Tiny fought to get a big, black cloth sack over the fawn's head. Once an animal can't see, it usually calms down.

Finally he got it over the top of the deer's head and ears. The little guy quit trying to kick.

With the head not flailing around so much, Tiny could wrap a towel around its eyes, a blindfold. Then he opened the black sack in such a way that the fawn's nose stuck out in the air. It was a slick arrangement, and Tiny really knew how to make it work.

He reached for the dressings on the lower shelf of the table. "Mrs. Dexter here found the fawn in her front yard this morning."

"Wow. What happened to it?"

"Dogs, I suppose," Mrs. Dexter said. She had a soft, pretty voice to go with her soft, pretty face. "I heard a commotion before dawn, but I didn't see this little fellow until I went out for the paper."

"You live on a farm?" I asked. I always wanted to live on a real farm. My dad grew up on a farm.

"Edge of town. Just a little place. But we like it."

Some of the fawn's rips and gashes were huge. I never would have thought dogs could do all that.

Tiny paused from bandaging big gashes in the fawn's rump. He pointed to the far corner. "Les, we're almost out of Ace bandages. See if you can find something in that cabinet."

"Ace bandages are those tan, stretchy things, right?"

He grunted something as I hurried over to paw through the cabinet. I wasn't the first person looking for something and leaving the shelves all messed up. In fact, it was such a jumble I just started dumping stuff out on the floor. I found a couple of boxed Ace bandages way in back.

I brought them to Tiny. "I think these are all."

"They won't be enough. There's bed sheets in the cupboard left of the sink. We can tear one of them into strips."

I knew who the "we" was going to be. I dug out a sheet, found scissors to start each tear with, and ripped sheet-long strips about the width of the Ace bandages. Three inches or so. I would much rather have been helping with the fawn, but this had to be done.

Half an hour later, we finally finished. The fawn was all trussed up and bandaged and tucked into a big floor cage. The woman complimented Tiny and left.

Tiny looked beat. He flopped into a chair and let his arms and legs sprawl.

"Mike usually helps you," I said. "Where is he?"

"Out working with his brothers. He says he's gonna get rich. He wants lots of money. I said, 'You ain't gonna get wealthy by weeding flower beds.' And he says, 'Not by giving my time away at the shelter, either.' So he hasn't been around for a few days."

I flopped in a chair, too. "But you aren't the only person who volunteers."

"No, but two of them are on vacation. Tiff sprained her ankle playing softball. Mrs. Forster had to go to a wedding. And that

Tammy somebody was here one day, saw the blood and guts, and decided not to do it."

I hopped back up, in no mood to goof off. "Well, those blood and guts are all over the place today. I'll start cleaning up. I'll do the tables first and then the floor."

Tiny lurched to his feet. "I'll get the food dishes filled. It's past feeding time."

So I spritzed all the gurneys and exam tables with disinfectant spray and cleaned them off. It took a while. Some of the blood smears and fur bits were dried on hard.

I called across the room, "How come so many animals are inside here? You usually put them in outdoor cages after you take care of them."

"Dr. Meyers hasn't seen them yet. She got called out to a farm. A pack of dogs or something ripped up a farmer's sheep."

Maybe living on a farm wasn't such a hot ticket after all.

Tiny crossed the long room with an armload of dog dishes from the dishwasher. "I'm sure glad you're here. How'd you know I needed you?"

"Well, it's this way—" I paused for dramatic effect "—I'm going to become a great chef. I suppose if I were cooking for four hundred people, I'd be busy most of the day. But cooking at home seems to be a once-in-a-while thing, so I had time on my hands."

"Then I can sure take some off your hands for you. We're behind with a lot of stuff around here."

We filled the food dishes and loaded them into the beat-up old coaster wagon. Then we went out to feed the animals in the outside cages. It's an old farm, this rescue shelter. The main part is in the Quonset hut sort of building, where we'd just been. But most animals and birds were housed in chicken wire cages out in the farmyard. Many, many cages, most on rickety two-by-four legs. Feeding all those animals is a kick; you give each one just enough of the exact kind of food it needs. It's an art.

I didn't tell Tiny that I had been bored spitless this morning and that coming out here to see him was an act of desperation. My big sister Hannah went to the mall with some other shopping freaks. Not-as-big-sister Catherine went up the street to a friend's house. I crossed the street to see if Bits wanted to play Monopoly, but she was all wrapped up in a computer game and didn't want to. Lynn wasn't home. And when I called Tiny's house, no one answered, so I figured he was out here.

But I enjoyed working and taking care of animals, especially in a sort of animal hospital like this. What really surprised me, though, was that so many of the cages outside were full. It looked like there'd been a Texas chain saw massacre without Texas or chain saws.

I watched a really mangled bunny nibble at carrot greens. "What happened to all these poor beasts?"

Tiny paused beside me, watching the rabbit. "Some say wolves."

3

I hungered for adventure. I hungered for the great outdoors. Actually, I hungered to goof off somewhere, because, if I stayed home, I'd end up mowing the lawn. I called Bits. She was busy. I called Lynn. She felt like going to Sugar Creek Park. So I rode my bike out there with her.

As we crossed Crestline, I yelled to her, "Dad says that out beyond town, Sugar Creek still has farms all along it, just like the old days."

"My father says it's big enough to be a river more than a creek," Lynn called back to me. "You haven't been here in the spring, yet. Wait till you see it during the spring melt, especially when it rains."

"Really howling, huh?" Someday, I decided, I would travel the length of Sugar Creek from its beginning to its end.

Today, though, we merely went to the park. Within the town, Sugar Creek County Park cut a broad swath of green trees and brush right through some of the nicest neighborhoods. The park was a couple miles long and maybe half a mile wide or a little less; that's quite a swath. A chain-link fence separated the park from the homes and lawns. Deep inside its cool, quiet woods, nature trails laced in and out along the creek. It's a peaceful place. Pleasant. And enough interesting animals live there that you never get bored.

We locked our bikes to the rack in the picnic area at the west park entrance. We hung our helmets on the handlebars, because who wants to tote a "brain basket" all over? Then we went for a nature stroll.

Did I say "peaceful"? About a quarter mile back along the main trail, we heard shouting up ahead. It sounded like a man and woman, not just kids messing around.

I broke into a run toward the noise, with Lynn right behind me. Who would be screaming like that? Beyond the Swamp Loop side trail, we came upon two grown-up hikers in shorts and lug sole shoes. The woman, with blonde hair cut short, sniffled, and I realized she was crying.

She stood staring down at her husband. He was kneeling. And in front of him lay a fawn. A bloody fawn. But it was still alive.

He wagged his head. "I don't know what we can do for it. It will die, I'm sure."

"Maybe not, sir." I stepped up to them. "A friend of ours volunteers at a wild animal rescue shelter. Yesterday we patched one up that was hurt as bad as this one. I called Tiny this morning, and it's still alive. We can take this one there."

He stood up, looking disgusted. "Well, you can waste time on it if you want, but I say it's not worth messing with. It's going to die."

"George!" the woman exploded, half furious and still half crying. "If there's a chance of saving it, we're going to try!"

It was sure obvious that George didn't think much of trying. But what could he do? He picked up the fawn, trying to keep it at arm's length but couldn't. It got blood all over him, and that seemed to *really* fry his eggs. Just as angry as the blonde woman, he stomped back on the trail toward the picnic area parking lot, as the fawn struggled weakly in his arms.

Lynn and I followed.

By the time he got to his car, his shirt and shorts were a mess. He was all sweaty, too. It's hard work carrying a deer, even one that small. "A fine walk this turned out to be!" Grump, grump, grump.

I thought about the woman who had brought the fawn in yesterday. She had gotten all smeared and dirty, too, but she never seemed to notice. The fawn had been the important thing to her. I liked her attitude better than this man's.

Lynn and I explained to them how to get to the rescue shelter. Since his clothes were a mess anyway, George was elected to hold the deer while his wife drove. They offered to take us along, but neither one of us was allowed to get in a car with strangers. So we just rode our bikes out there as fast as we could.

We got there only about five minutes after they did. I think they might have gotten a little lost.

George's day was definitely not going well.

The fawn had made a further mess on him. And when they got inside, he saw this kid less than twelve in charge of the whole place.

George blew up. He roared about incompetence. He threatened to call the police and the Humane Society and the Game and Fish Department. Nobody bothered to tell him the Game and Fish Department licensed the shelter to keep game birds and animals. Nobody explained to him that the place operated with the blessing of the Humane Society, or even that the police themselves often brought in injured animals.

We ignored him because we were all working on the fawn. Quickly and expertly, Tiny trussed it up and blindfolded it. He got the blonde lady to work with him. It was amazing. She changed instantly from a weeping, sorrowful woman to an eager helper. She really seemed to enjoy the work, messy and sad as it was.

Finally, we had done all we could. Tiny put the fawn in a plastic clothes basket in the corner under a table, because he was out of cages.

The woman wandered about the room, peering from cage to cage. "I never realized so many animals get hurt."

"It's not usually this busy. We have a sort of rush going on," Tiny said. "Dog-bite sort of injuries."

George frowned. "The wolves?"

Tiny and I looked at each other. I said, "A lady in here yesterday claims wolves attacked a deer."

Tiny added, "And the vet who takes care of our animals here was busy most of yesterday stitching a farmer's flock back together. The farmer said it was wolves."

George snorted. "Yeah! That's what we saw, all right! A pack of wolves. They couldn't be anything else. The leader was this big!" And he held his hand three feet off the floor.

"Wolves come in different colors, don't they?" the lady asked.

Tiny nodded. "I think light gray through black. But I'll have to look it up. I'm not sure."

"One of them was brown. Actually, more like tan. A baby. But it was definitely wolves."

Mrs. Ferguson, the afternoon and evening volunteer, showed up then. The adults all introduced themselves and started talking. In an instant they completely forgot about us kids. So the three of us went outside.

We sat down in the grass beside the bikes. Tiny looked just plain pooped.

Lynn frowned. "What's all this about wolves?"

I bobbed my head toward Tiny. "You're the naturalist with the binoculars around your neck half the time. You know all this stuff. It isn't wolves, is it?"

"Wolves?" Lynn asked.

Tiny wagged his head. "Don't see how it could be. It could be a coyote, though. A family of coyotes. They're around here, and there's getting to be more of them. Yeah, that's probably it. Coyotes."

I grunted. "You off tomorrow?"

"At last. Been here all week."

"Know where we want to go tomorrow?"

"Yeah. For ice cream."

"Good idea. Also to the natural history museum. I bet they'll know if wolves are here."

Lynn repeated, "Wolves? Here?"

Tiny stared straight ahead a few moments, seeing nothing. He licked his lips. "Les? There's so many people around here. Families. Kids. What if it *is* wolves? Do you suppose they'd bite a child?"

4

Our family was eating breakfast the next morning (I with my favorite, a ham sandwich and an orange—but eaten separately, not at the same time—when Catherine asked, "So what are your plans today, Squirt?"

I don't suppose I even have to mention that "Squirt" is her most commonly used term of address to me.

"I," I announced grandly, "am going to explore the intriguing prospect that a pack of wolves has invaded the county. And maybe, this very moment, they are ravaging some innocent kitten." I said that because she loved cats.

"You're sick. You are very, very sick." She continued eating her ordinary breakfast of cereal and toast.

Dad cocked an eyebrow. "Wolves?"

I got serious with Dad, since he always wanted to know where I was going. "Tiny's shelter is running over with animals that have been all bitten up. And a couple people say they saw wolves. So Tiny and Lynn and I are going over to the natural history museum to ask the curator there about wolves."

"Good idea. Back by lunch?"

"Yes, sir."

You know, that wasn't a bad thing—Dad's

always knowing where I was. If something nasty ever happened, he'd know about where to start looking for me, and when. So when he asked, I didn't resent it, the way some kids do. He wasn't checking up; he was just keeping track.

Hannah was staring at me, wide-eyed. "There really are wolves? Do they really eat cats?"

"Tiny thinks it's coyotes. I'll let you know."

I finished my orange. The doorbell rang, so I tossed the peel into the trash, grabbed my helmet, and hit the road. Not literally. I try desperately *not* to hit any roads, especially when on roller blades.

Lynn was all smiles as she climbed aboard her bike. "I love going to the museum."

"Me too."

A girl's voice called to us. Bits stood on her porch, across the street. "Where you going?"

We pulled into her yard. I said, "Natural history museum. Tiny's coming, too. Come along, why don't you?"

"When you coming home?"

"Lunch." I glanced at Lynn. She nodded.

"Can I use your computer till then?"

I was about to say yes, but Lynn burst out with, "Oh, please, Bits! Your father chased you out of the house and said, 'Go do something outside on a nice day like this.' Right?"

"None of your business!"

"You and your computer games." Lynn wagged her head.

I suggested, "Come along. You can hole up

in the museum's computer room and play rain forest population games while we talk to people about wolves."

"Why wolves?"

"Why not wolves?" I tooled my bike out across the yard and bumped down off the curb. I practiced trying to do wheelies while she got her bike. Notice, I did not say *practiced doing wheelies*. I said *practiced trying*, because that's all the farther I could get.

Then Bits rolled out onto the street, and we were on our way.

The natural history museum is on the north side of Metro Park. When we got there, Tiny's and Mike's bikes were locked to the rack outside the museum's huge front doors. I was glad to see Mike's bike there. He spent an awful lot of his life working harder than many men, and he was the youngest kid in the Sugar Creek Gang. Maybe today he could relax and have some fun.

Bits headed straight as an arrow for the museum's kid section and its computers. Lynn, Tiny, Mike, and I walked back to the education director at the end of the hall, and she called the mammal curator for us.

Yes, he could talk to us a few minutes. She smiled and directed us up a flight of stairs, past the hall of mammals and the marine displays. Did you know a humpback whale suspended from the ceiling can fill the length of a very big hall? The four of us paused a moment to look straight up, gaping. Imagine being in a whaleboat a hundred years ago, harpooning one of those things, and away it goes. And you're hanging on to the end of a puny, little old rope attached to it.

The curator looked like how you think a professor ought to look. Slightly built and slim, he hid behind a really neat beard. A few gray hairs in the beard and around his ears were the only sign that he was probably older than Dad, and that's *old!*

"Dr. Owen Morgan." He introduced himself and offered his hand. Tiny shook hands and introduced himself, Lynn, Mike, and me. I felt curiously important and grown up.

Tiny explained his job. He told about the animals. Then he said something I didn't know until then. "The wolves—or whatever they are—are doing a lot of damage. Almost three-fourths of the animals that come to us end up dying."

Three-fourths! That really slapped me.

Dr. Morgan nodded. "Let's go out to the dioramas."

It had never occurred to me, but the curator probably knew every detail of every display lining the walls of the Mammal Hall. He led us directly to a scene showing Arctic tundra.

I love dioramas. Those are those displays behind glass with stuffed animals in natural poses and set up in their natural habitat. The plants all around in the foreground look real. A painting of the scenery, arcing around the background, makes it seem you're really there.

The tundra one had snow as the base, with

some rocks sticking out. Green and gray lichens on the rocks were the only plants. Wolves were attacking a circle of musk oxen. The display had only one mounted musk ox. The others were painted on the backdrop. But the five snarling, slinking wolves were all mounts.

"See how the running wolves are holding their tails?" Dr. Morgan asked.

"Straight out," Mike said. "They do that for real?"

"Yes. Now come down here to the desert scene." Dr. Morgan led the way. In the desert diorama, quail and a jackrabbit squatted behind a bush as a coyote trotted by. A snake, two peccaries (wild, piglike animals), and a mule deer watched it all.

Lynn pointed. "The coyote's tail droops."

Dr. Morgan smiled. "Exactly. When the animal is moving, if it holds its tail straight out, you're watching a wolf. If it holds its tail at a downward slope, it's a coyote."

I pointed, too. "But this coyote is a lot smaller than those wolves."

"True, but it's hard to judge size at a distance. From a hundred yards away, they'll seem nearly the same size, unless you see them together. And you won't. Coyotes and wolves don't run together."

"I read that coyotes are extending their range—spreading out into areas where they didn't used to be," Tiny said. "Are wolves?"

"No. Especially not here in the lower forty-eight." By that, I knew Dr. Morgan meant the states other than Alaska and Hawaii.

Tiny stared at the mounted coyote a few moments. "Do coyotes ever go after livestock? Farm animals?"

"Rarely. Usually, if you see them with a dead farm animal, it was dead when they found it. They'll scavenge domestic animals."

Mike asked, "Do they eat rabbits and squirrels?"

"Yes, indeed. Small mammals are their preferred food, but they'll eat just about anything humans eat—and a whole lot that's downright repulsive to humans. Carrion. Green nuts."

Mike started looking worried. "They ever attack . . . you know . . . kids? Little kids?" Mike is short for his age.

Dr. Morgan laughed. "Almost never. I can't think of a single instance of coyotes attacking a person. There are stories that wolves used to a hundred years ago, but not coyotes. You're safe."

And at that, Mike looked embarrassed.

"I doubt, though, that your problem is wolves." Dr. Morgan absent-mindedly scratched his beard. "I'd go more for feral dogs. They can actually be more dangerous than wolves or coyotes. They have no fear of humans."

Mike frowned. "What's 'feral'?"

"A domestic animal that has gone wild. For example, people don't want their dog anymore, so they dump it along a country road. It learns to live off the land, out in the wild. Pretty soon, it doesn't need people. That's feral."

Lynn added, "I've heard of feral house cats."

Dr. Morgan nodded. "Many of those, and they do terrible damage to wild birds."

Tiny asked some more questions, but I wasn't listening closely. Now that we knew how to tell coyotes and wolves apart, we were ready for the next step. The next step was to *see* the animals. But they seemed to be hitting all over the area—a farm here, a subdivision there, Sugar Creek Park—there didn't appear to be any pattern. Where would we go to find them?

And why in the world would anyone in his right mind deliberately go out looking to get face to face with a wolf?

5

Want to hear about one of the world's great coincidences? And I mean world-class, all the way. Now it's true, our downtown Metro Park was world-class, just as great as New York's Central Park, which I have visited. All it lacked is the zoo. And, like Central Park, it had a world-class natural history museum on one side and a big art museum on the other side. The coincidence was: Right next to our natural history museum was the world's greatest ice cream stand. Now is that planning or what?

The result of this coincidence: Less than ten minutes after we left Dr. Morgan, the five of us were sitting around a table under an umbrella in Metro Park, licking away at the world's greatest ice cream.

Bits scowled. "I would have won if I could have played that population program another twenty minutes. You guys shouldn't have pulled me away from it." But then she brightened noticeably as she dug into her maple nut sundae with extra whipped cream.

"No, you wouldn't." Tiny examined his raspberry hot fudge sundae from all four sides—figuring out how to tackle it, I guess. "It's rigged so you can't beat that one. All six species end up going extinct. I know. I tried all day on it once."

"You weren't doing it right, then." Bits started working on her ice cream in earnest. "Nobody invents a game you can't win."

Tiny shook his head. "That's the whole point of it, don't you see? Everything eventually goes extinct. The only thing you can do with that game is stretch out the species life a little longer."

"Wrong. You can beat it. I'm sure you can beat it."

Then it got real quiet as we all wallowed in the rich flavors of the world's finest treat.

I took a big slurp off my peanut butter chocolate chip cone. "I've decided I'm going to be a naturalist when I grow up. Like Dr. Morgan there. Can you imagine going to work every day in that museum? I mean, you walk past those dioramas, and when a stuffed bird or something falls out of its tree, you go in and put it back up. And you know everything in the whole museum."

With his tongue out as far as it could go, Mike trimmed the edge of his double-dip chocolate cone. "Tiny already does."

"Do not." Tiny dipped a big spoonful. "But someday I'm gonna."

Lynn paused to savor a spoonful of her French vanilla butterscotch sundae. Then, "I'm glad you got the day off, Mike."

"Didn't get the day off." Mike slurped his cone again. "I quit. My stingy brother don't pay me enough money doing that yard work."

Lynn smiled. "So you're going to go wolf hunting with us?"

"Nope. Got a real job."

Bits frowned. "You do not! Who'd hire a ten-year-old? It's not legal."

Mike looked smug as a cat with canary feathers in its whiskers. "Gonna help at a pet-grooming shop. Sweep up and stuff. Five dollars an hour!"

Bits growled, "Liar."

"Am not!"

Lynn wasn't smiling anymore. "That pet shop on Eleventh Street?"

Mike nodded. "They board animals, so I'll help out in the kennels and the salon both. Feed and clean. 'Zackly the same as I did at the rescue shelter for free, only I get paid. He hired me 'cause I'm experienced."

"Paid how?"

"Cash! Gonna be rolling in money real soon. I start Monday."

"Five dollars an hour." Lynn looked at her sundae as if counting the crushed peanuts on it, then began eating again.

It sounded like a fortune to me, but I knew Bits had a point. The only job a kid our age could legally hold was stuff like delivering newspapers or working on a farm. But if Mike said he was working, he was. He never lied about things.

"Oh, hey," I said. "Before I forget. You guys are all invited to my place tomorrow for Sunday dinner. Roast turkey and the trimmings."

"Why turkey?" Bits grabbed a paper napkin that was blowing. "It's not Thanksgiving."

"If you must know, it was on special. I'm going to be a great chef if I don't become a naturalist, and I'm fixing it."

Tiny grinned. "*You're* cooking? Quick! We all gotta think of some excuse to stay away!"

Bits scraped the sides of her plastic sundae bowl. "I'm busy. I'm gonna make sure I'm busy."

Lynn licked her spoon. "I have to wash my hair. Maybe two or three times. It's very dirty."

It was not.

"I have to sort my socks. Organize my sock drawer." Mike bit into his cone. "Black on the left and white on the right."

"Oh, come on, guys!"

Lynn laughed. "Relax, Les. Of course we'll come. We want to. We have to see if you have the makings of a great chef. If this is going to be anything like those cookies we tried to bake once, it will certainly be entertaining. You do have a fresh battery in the smoke alarm, don't you?"

Tiny snorted. "Entertaining, yeah, but we'll starve."

My friends are a whole herd of clowns. I brought the conversation back to the subject at hand. "So where are we going to find wolves?"

"I've been thinking about that." Lynn pointed up the street. "Let's get a county map at the drugstore. They sell them on a rack right by the checkout stand. And mark all the places someone saw the wolves. Or coyotes."

"Hey, yeah!" Tiny grinned. "If they have a home range, maybe we can figure it out."

So when we finished, we pooled our money. Ice cream treats sure make a big, big dent in funds. We didn't have enough for a postcard, let alone a map.

"No problem," said Lynn. "I'm sure that tourist information kiosk out by the freeway has them."

I would not in a million years have thought of that. But we biked out to the kiosk—staying on back streets as usual—and there they were. A whole rack of county maps. We took one map but didn't pick up any of the many brochures that tell visitors about the parks and restaurants and museums. Lynn even signed the guest register.

We called my mom. She was cooking pork chops for dinner, and, yes, there was enough for company. So then we stopped by Tiny's and Mike's houses and asked their moms if they could eat at my place. Yes, but be home by dark.

We rode on past my door to Lynn's. Her mom said OK. We were going to get permission for Bits, but she decided she wanted to eat at home and left us. Lynn wagged her head sadly as Bits put her bike away and went inside.

Dinner wasn't ready yet, so we could spread the map out on the kitchen table. I got out my colored markers.

We all leaned on the map on our elbows, staring at it and not knowing beans what we were looking at.

Lynn pointed. "This is the rescue shelter, here. Right?"

"Right!" Tiny took the black marker and made a little circle. "No wolves reported near us."

"If they *were* near there," Mike asked, "do you s'pose the smell of all the injured animals would lure them in close?"

"Probably, yeah. So they don't likely prowl around that area."

"Here's the park." I pointed. "We know they came there." It wasn't that tough a thing to find, considering that the parks were coded in green and there was this huge green block labeled *Sugar Creek County Park* west of Crestline.

Tiny put a big red spot in it.

The woman who brought the fawn in had filled out a facility-use card. Tiny sort of remembered her address and made a big red mark there too. He also remembered where the farmer whose sheep were attacked lived. He marked there.

"Way cool!" Mike cooed. "Look at that!"

And he was right, it *was* cool. The red spots were clustered in a big loose circle, ragged-edged but obvious.

Tiny stood up straight and nodded. "There's their home range, then. There's where we go wolf hunting."

6

Someday the newspaper headline will read:

Les Walker, World's Greatest Chef, Visits City

And the newspaper would be the *Seattle Times* or maybe the *Post Intelligencer*, because I'm from Seattle originally. That's home. We had just moved halfway across the country to this house because Dad switched jobs to a new law firm. This house didn't feel completely like home yet.

I took the turkey out of the refrigerator and set it on the counter. (You know, don't you, that you always, *always* thaw frozen chickens and turkeys in the fridge and never out in the room. Poultry and poultry products such as eggs carry germs, *salmonella* bacteria specifically. I mean, they nearly all do. And if the bacteria count builds high enough, the way it can at room temperature, you can get food poisoning from it. Also, do you realize how hard it is to work *salmonella* into an ordinary conversation like this?)

While I fought that massive beast, I wondered if maybe, when I went back to Seattle someday for a visit, they'd have a parade for me. I couldn't remember right off if I ever heard of a great chef getting a "welcome home" parade. But then I couldn't think of any great naturalists getting a parade, either.

The turkey was heavy and cold. I groped around inside. The body cavity was *really* cold.

"Mom? I can't find any heart or gizzard or liver."

Mom was making potato soup for lunch. "In a store turkey, they're in a little bag where the craw was removed."

The craw. The craw. That was a sacklike place in birds' gullets—their throats—where they store food. I dug under the flap of skin up front, and wouldn't you know, there was the bag. "Do I stuff this hole too?"

"Sometimes. Usually not."

Hannah came in with a tray. She had just set the table for lunch out on the deck. "I think it's really interesting what God did in church this morning."

"What's that?" Mom asked.

"You know. Here's Les, all hot to catch wolves, and where does the pastor preach? Luke 10:3. I mean, there are only thirteen verses in the whole Bible that mention wolves, and bingo."

Aha! Obviously, she had just looked up *wolves* in a concordance and counted the verses where it occurred. Also obviously, she was very smug about knowing all this.

Well, aha right back. I was one up on her. "Ah, my sweet sister. Of those thirteen, the ones that are *wolves of evening* don't count, because that's how somebody translated the

Hebrew word for hyenas. Wolves of evening are really hyenas."

Mom raised an eyebrow. "Now where'd you learn that? I'm impressed."

"There's this great computer program that's like a concordance only better. Goes into a lot of detail with pictures and everything."

"Computer. I should have known."

"Hey, at least I don't play computer games all day. Lynn says she's starting to worry about Bits. Bits spends too much time on games, she says." You don't realize how many slices there are in a loaf of bread until you have to tear up every one of them into little pieces.

"Know what you are?" Hannah glared at me. "An intellectual snob." And she marched out with the tray of extra stuff—salt, pepper, butter, rolls. When she can't win on points, she calls her little brother names.

Mom chopped me an onion for the stuffing when she chopped one for the soup. She seemed to be in deep thought. "So Lynn has noticed it, too. I think Bits's father is getting worried about her. He blocked certain Web sites off-limits for her, but he's concerned anyway."

But my mind was working on other things. "Mom? I hate to admit it, but Hannah has a point. I mean, was God saying something to me when the pastor talked about wolves today? If it's a coincidence, it's sure a weird coincidence. I guess what I'm saying is, how do you know when God is telling you something and when it's something else?"

She smiled at me. "Do you realize what you are doing?"

"Yeah. I'm mixing the torn-up bread with the chopped onion and garlic and sage and savory and thyme, like you said. Shouldn't I?"

Mom laughed. "No, that's right. Keep going. I mean, you are asking a theological question people have asked since time began. Exactly how is God speaking to us, if at all, and what is He saying?"

"Yeah! That's it!" I added milk and chicken bouillon to the bowlful of dry stuff. Stirring got a lot harder instantly. "So? What's the answer?"

"I don't have one. Each person is different. So God speaks to each in a unique way. Do you understand what I'm saying?"

"Yeah." My arm was getting tired from trying to mix that glop.

"Good. Then give me an example to illustrate what I just said." My mother, the teacher.

"I just scoop a handful and shove it in, right?" I had seen Mom stuff a chicken many a time. I assumed stuffing the turkey was the same.

"Right."

I thought about an example as I worked.

And it *was* work. Raw stuffing just doesn't cooperate. The goo escaped being pushed in by squeezing out between my fingers. It globbed and pasted up all over my hand. And my arm. For a while there, I had more on me than I had in the turkey. "I don't have quite enough to fill the whole inside. Does that matter?"

"Nope."

"An example. Like, when God announced the birth of Jesus, a star was enough to tell the wise men with. But He had to hit the shepherds over the head with a choir of angels."

When Mom laughs, her whole body gets into the act. It's the neatest thing. The noise of laughter exploded out, her hands flew up, her back arched.

She finally got back to being serious. "Listen to what God would tell you, Les. But also listen for ways He might do it. And I'm proud of you that you care enough to want to hear Him."

Dad came in waving the Sunday paper. "Did you see this, Les?"

"No, I'm too busy cooking. I didn't even get to read the comics yet." I slipped the turkey into the oven. That doesn't sound hard. But remember that, when it was stuffed, that old bird weighed almost a fourth of what I weighed.

"Some newspaper reporter got wind of the wolf rumors. Big picture story here. They interviewed farmers about the ravaged sheep and deer. Lots of quotes."

"Wow! They mention Tiny? He knows more about it than anybody."

"No. Too bad, too. I don't know how much of this is hype, but it sounds like they're taking your wolves very seriously."

7

Dad and some friends went sailing a couple times when he was in college. He says that sailing is hours of boredom punctuated by a few moments of terror. Cooking is something like that, too. After I hurry–hurry–hurried to truss up the turkey and put it in the oven, there wasn't much left to do for five hours.

Then the phone rang, and my afternoon was instantly saved from boredom.

It was Tiny. "Hey, Les! Want to come along with Dr. Meyers and me? We're going out to a farm to take care of some animals."

"Yeah! Where do I meet you?"

"We'll pick you up at your house in ten minutes. Bring a raincoat. It's raining. And call Lynn and Bits."

I did that. Lynn was on my doorstep almost before her phone receiver went *click*.

Bits said she didn't have time. Her father yelled something in the background that I couldn't make out. She said, "Yeah, I'll come." So it sounded like her father was chasing her outdoors again. In the rain, yet.

Veterinarian Helen Meyers's van pulled up at our door, and the three of us piled in, all wrapped up in slickers. Tiny and Mike were in the front seat with Dr. Meyers.

Tiny twisted around in his seat belt shoulder harness. "Dr. Meyers asked me to give her a hand and asked if I knew anyone else who could help."

"Thanks for remembering us!" and I meant it, too!

And so Dr. Meyers showed up at this farm with five noble assistants. The Sugar Creek Gang.

The farmer, a big, blond, hefty guy, was waiting for us by his barn door. He seemed the kind of man who would be cheerful and always smiling, but he looked grim now.

His wife, in blue jeans and a T-shirt, stood beside him. Her eyes were all wet and red and puffy. She had been crying.

Dr. Meyers introduced us to them. Their names were Bob and Jan Bradhurst. But they weren't in a mood to be casual.

"This way." Mr. Bradhurst wheeled abruptly and led us to a nearby shed. It was obviously a poultry shed. It had a regular door for people, and on the side was a door for birds. A ramp led from that door down into a big, bare, fenced in yard.

What caught my attention was the size of that bird door—bigger by far than a chicken would need.

Mr. Bradhurst opened the people door. Bits was the first to step inside. I heard her cry out, "Oh, no!"

The farmer grimaced. "There's this mess, and there's the sheep and a couple calves."

Dr. Meyers glanced inside and nodded. "Les, you and Bits triage the turkey shed here with Jan. Tiny, you and Mike and Lynn come with me." As she hurried off, I heard her say, "Tiny, you and Mike will help Bob with the sheep. Lynn and I will see to the calves."

Triage. I knew what that meant. You have a lot of injuries in one place, so you sort them into minor, major, and horrible. But you tend to the major ones first, because the victims with the horrible injuries will almost certainly die anyway, so you spend your time where it's most likely to save the person. When Mom learned that, she said it sounded heartless, but I can see the sense of it.

Bits and Mrs. Bradhurst and I stood in the middle of this big turkey house, looking at disaster. The house was just one big room with perches all around the walls. Skylights made it very light, and a turbine vent whirred in the roof, keeping it fairly cool. It smelled bad—but then, you don't expect a turkey shed to be a bed of roses. I learned, though, that when turkeys are very upset, they do unspeakable things.

Most of the turkeys, dozens of them, were nothing but big piles of motionless feathers. Another couple dozen had been mauled badly. Their white feathers were dirty and all bloody. That left just a few that were still alive and unhurt.

Mrs. Bradhurst started to weep silently. "They're stupid birds, but they were so friendly. So—"

Bits was the first to snap out of it. "Let's throw all the dead ones over by the door, just for now. Mrs. Bradhurst, can we chase the ones that aren't hurt out into the yard?"

And that moment, Mrs. Bradhurst stuffed her sorrow aside somewhere that it didn't show. "Yes. Yes, of course. Not that one. Its wing is half bitten off. Not that one, either."

It took us awhile. We caught each turkey and looked it over, because some had blood on them even though they weren't hurt. It was just plain hard work. A big turkey can weigh over thirty pounds. That's OK if you're a sumo wrestler. It goes without saying that we weren't.

As soon as the healthy ones had been chased outside, we closed the poultry door. Then we dragged the dead ones over and piled them by the people door. Two of the injured ones died right in front of us.

"Chickens and turkeys stress easily," Mrs. Bradhurst explained. "If they're terribly upset or their environment is bad for too long, they just keel over."

"This is stress, all right." Bits was sweating.

The summer before this, back in Washington state, Mom enrolled me in a summer enrichment program at my school: first aid. We learned to dress cuts and bandage them, splint fractures, and perform mouth-to-mouth resuscitation.

And no, you better believe I did *not* do mouth-to-mouth on a turkey. But we splinted and bandaged them aplenty.

Mrs. Bradhurst brought a couple buckets of water. We sponged blood off, applied dressings and bandages, and taped popsicle-stick splints to broken wings and legs. It was absolutely the weirdest hour I ever spent in my whole life.

That was only the first aid. We knew that when Dr. Meyers got done with the sheep and calves, she would come here to administer *second* aid, you might say.

We hauled all the dozens of dead birds out the door. Then Mrs. Bradhurst drew a shade across the skylights. The big room turned dim. Darkness, she explained, would help them calm down.

We stepped outside, closing the door behind us. And I realized just then how much I had been missing fresh, odorless air. I just stood there awhile, breathing in and out. Mrs. Bradhurst ran off to help the others.

Bits stood beside me in the light rain, staring at the bedraggled mound of dead birds. The rain made those rumpled, ratty feathers even rattier. "You know what 'cold turkey' means, don't you?"

"Yeah." I couldn't keep my eyes off them either. "When you're addicted to something and you all at once quit whatever it is without any help. Or you don't taper off or anything."

"Well, here's a new meaning for it. Dead cold turkeys."

Along with the others, Bits and I followed Dr. Meyers around, helping where we could.

She gave injections to animals and to some of the turkeys. She quickly and gently tended injuries. She peered into eyes and mouths and ears and somehow guessed exactly what she needed to know about their health. Very mysterious.

I decided then that if being a famous chef didn't pan out, I might be a veterinarian. In fact, by the time we climbed into the van, being a vet had edged ahead of chef as a career choice.

We would get back to town around five, I figured. Just in time for the gang to troop into my house, clean up, and sit down to a turkey feast.

No, our afternoon didn't really dull my appetite for turkey, and that's strange to me. But you somehow don't associate those big, fluffy white birds with the roasted bird in front of you. They don't look enough alike, I guess, and the ones in feathers still have heads and feet.

Besides, this was going to be the feast of the century. Well, maybe the decade. Year? Last twelve hours, at least.

"This dinner better be good, Les," Bits said.

"Delicious!" I crowed. "I wrapped the bird in foil, and it's been stewing in its own juices ever since church."

"Your mom's keeping an eye on this, I hope."

"Nope," I said proudly, "she told me I'm on my own. She and the girls had to go to some kind of shower with the church women this afternoon. This is *my* creation, beginning to end. I did the potatoes and corn myself."

"Gravy?" Bits didn't look at all convinced.

I grinned, pretty sheepish. "Out of a can. Hey, I'm not a pro yet, OK?" At home, I hurried to the kitchen.

I had it all planned out. I would put the potatoes and creamed corn, both already partly cooked, in the oven. I'd unwrap the bird and brown it for another twenty minutes or so. Then it would all be ready to go on the table at once. Slick, huh?

I saw that Mom had gotten back. She was in the kitchen, looking bleak.

"Hi, Mom." I frowned. "Didn't your get-together this afternoon go all right?"

"It went fine. Uh, Les . . ."

I popped the oven door open. No heat rushed out.

Mom stepped up beside me at the stove. "The oven has two controls, Les. This one sets the temperature. And that other one turns it on. To bake something, you have to set them both. I'm sorry."

I had adjusted the temperature control just fine. But I hadn't touched that other dial.

The oven was still cold and always had been.

So was the turkey.

8

The Bradhurst farm disaster made the national news. They showed pictures of the dead livestock all tossed onto a huge heap in the rain. It looked so sad and dismal. They showed the bandaged calves, the splinted turkeys. In fact, they showed a closeup of a turkey that I, Les Walker, had personally treated (they didn't mention my name, of course). Then they ran footage of wolves from some nature show while they guessed about who could do all that damage.

It's not a nice way to get on the national news.

Monday morning, Lynn and I went out on our bikes into that circle our map had defined, looking for wolves. It probably won't surprise you to learn that we didn't see any. In the afternoon, we biked out to the rescue shelter to help Tiny feed the animals. The shelter director had managed to round up a few more volunteers, but feeding was still a humongous job. Every single cage had animals or birds in it.

I hope Lynn becomes an ambassador when she grows up, because she's already as tactful as all get out. For instance, all that long day, she never once mentioned the cold turkey. She never once commented on the bucket of fried chicken that Dad went out and got. Actually, it went with the potatoes and corn just fine.

In contrast, my sisters could not be diplomats if their lives depended on it. I bet it will be years before they quit teasing me. If ever.

Lynn and I had helped out at the shelter more than once. The minute we arrived, we hustled right in and filled food dishes because Tiny was still busy cleaning out pens.

Then Tiny and Lynn and I fed all the animals. That was the fun part. After that we bagged over a dozen dead animals and put them in the Dumpster. That part wasn't fun, but it had to be done, so we did it.

I think sadness is a part of death. I mean, for instance, here was Jesus coming to raise His friend Lazarus, right? You remember the story. He knew what was going to happen. In fact, He thanked His Father God in advance. But when He first joined the mourners with Mary and Martha, all of them so sad, He wept, too. He knew He was going to sit down to supper with Lazarus, but He cried anyway. See what I mean? It's a package, so to speak.

The sadness was part of those dead animals also. Live animals are cute or funny or dangerous or huge or whatever. Think about bunnies and Kodiak bears. But dead animals are never cute or funny, no matter how lifelike some taxidermist tries to make them look. I don't know how to say it except that once they lost life, they . . . well . . . lost alive-ness. That eerie difference between life and death never shows in movies or TV. Death doesn't seem real there, especially when you're old enough to know that the actor is going to get up and walk away as soon as the camera stops.

I'd never really thought about that until we disposed of those dead animals.

We helped Tiny close up for the night. It was an important job, and I felt very grown-up doing it. We followed a list of things to do that was posted on the back of the front door. Lock up the supply closet. Check the back door. Turn out the lights. It was a long list.

The whole thing took maybe twenty minutes, because Tiny made certain we didn't skip an item. I'm sure that was why he was allowed to be in charge; he never goofed off or got sloppy.

He slipped his bird-watching binoculars around his neck as always. We climbed on our bikes then, the three of us, and headed home, single file along the country roads.

The shelter is a ways outside of town. Except for a few subdivisions—clusters of houses all clumped together with fields and woods around them—you're pretty much out in the weeds. By now we knew three or four ways to get to the shelter from our neighborhoods by using one set of country roads instead of another. Lynn was leading this evening. I noticed she was taking one of the longer ways.

We passed a gang of farmhands making hay. I love the smell of fresh hay. These folks were using a baler that stuffs the hay together and shapes it into a rectangular bundle. Some balers make a huge cylinder-shaped bale you have to pick up with a forklift. I like the rectangles better because, if you're big enough and strong enough, you can handle them all by yourself with just a couple hay hooks. Someday I'll be big enough and strong enough.

Tiny said, "Hard day." He trailed behind. Usually, he led.

Lynn said, "Oh, but it's beautiful. Feel how nicely it's cooled off already this evening. I love this time of year."

I said, "Hey! Stop! Look out there!" I pulled aside into the grass and jumped off my bike.

"What?" Tiny braked and laid his bike down in the deep grass of the roadside ditch. "Where?"

"Animals moving—way out there beyond the wheat field. You see them?" I pointed east.

A wire fence topped by a strand of barbed wire closed the wheat field away from the road. The wheat had already been combined; only the golden-brown stubble was left. Brambles and bushes covered the fence at the far side of the field, so you couldn't see very well into the overgrown pasture beyond it.

But you could see some movement. Half a dozen something were out there, and they weren't deer. Deer are tan. They weren't cows. Cows come in various colors but not these colors. It looked as if these were shades of gray.

Tiny bounded up onto the fence, sticking

the toes of his athletic shoes through the wire squares. He balanced himself by pressing a leg against the red steel fence post.

He whipped his binoculars up to his eyes.

"What is it?" Lynn asked. She climbed up on the fence on the other side of the post, but she swayed some.

I climbed onto the fence beside the next post down and shaded my eyes. "Can you see them?"

"Yeah." Tiny stood there, taller than tall because he was two feet off the ground up on that fence, and just watched. And watched. He breathed a word in an amazed tone of voice, but I couldn't hear what it was.

And then the animals moved along the far fence to a place where we could see them better. I could make out five. One of them, dark gray, had to be almost pony-sized. Three others, a little smaller than the big one, looked light gray with lighter faces. The smallest was a dull sort of brown.

"They're out in the open!" Lynn pointed excitedly. Despite being so shaky, she had climbed another couple strands.

They turned then and headed away from us, out across that overgrown pasture. The weeds and sumac and clumps of thistles swallowed them up.

We watched and waited awhile, but they didn't show themselves again.

I asked Tiny, "Could you see with your glasses how they carry their tails?"

"Yeah. Wolves carry their tails straight out, right?"

"Right."

"And coyotes carry theirs sloping down, right?"

"Yes." Carefully, Lynn stepped back off her perch.

Tiny jumped to the ground. He sounded almost scared. "I could only see the biggest one well. The grass was too high. It looked a lot like a wolf. But it held its tail sloping *up!*"

9

Early the next morning, Tiny and Mike met Lynn and me at Sugar Creek Park. We had decided to go on a serious wolf hunt.

Tiny spread out the county map on a picnic table near the park's trailhead. When he leaned over to look, the binoculars around his neck clunked on the table. "Where were we yesterday?"

"Nolan Road." Lynn studied the map a few moments, then ran her finger along a thin black line. "Would you say here, about?"

I nodded. "We had just crossed that dirt road there, remember? Where they were putting up hay." To tell the truth, I wasn't all that eager to go out looking for wolves. Not after we saw those animals out there that looked a whole lot like wolves. But I'd rather chew tin foil than admit I was scared, so I didn't say anything.

Mike looked a little uncomfortable, too, come to think of it. "Tiny told me all about those things you saw yesterday. That's awesome."

Lynn looked up from the map. "Tiny, did you tell anyone else about them? I mean anyone official?"

"Didn't have to." Tiny scowled. "They—the officials—seem to know all about it. More than all. You wouldn't believe some of the screwy stuff they said on TV last evening. Lies, false 'facts' . . ."

"So it was on local TV too." I wondered if God was speaking to me through more than just the pastor. "The paper had that piece on it, but then they're always looking for stuff to put in the Sunday paper, Dad says, because it's thicker."

And then, surprise, surprise. Here came Bits. She rolled her bike up to us and dumped it casually in the grass. "Your dad said you were all out wolf hunting, Lynn."

Lynn frowned. "When did you talk to my father?"

"This morning."

"But it's so early."

"I saw you leave, and then he came out to get his paper, and I said hello. Neighbors. You know."

"Four doors away." Now Lynn scowled. "Bits, did you ask him to let you use my computer?"

"Not exactly. Besides, Miss Selfish, don't you want anyone touching your precious mouse?" Bits looked at Tiny. "I thought you were working today."

"I called them and told them I wouldn't be in."

She dipped her head toward Mike. "How come you're not somewhere making five bucks an hour?"

"They got scared. They was afraid they'd get caught and have to pay a fine. They decided not to let me work there." Mike shrugged. "So I'm out of a job again. But I'll find another one. A better one."

"So you become a big game hunter instead." I turned back to the map. "Where we going to go?"

"I suggest out to Nolan Road again." Lynn plopped her helmet on her head. "Maybe explore that dirt road near where we saw them."

Tiny strapped his helmet on. "Look for tracks. If they've crossed that road, we'll know it."

Now that was exciting! I'd almost rather see tracks than the whole wolf.

Off we went. I sort of remembered that the sky was clear when I left the house. By now, and it wasn't very late in the morning at all, the blue had turned milky, and our shadows lost their sharp edges.

Tiny must have noticed, too. He said, "Bet it might rain this afternoon," as we paraded single file out onto Nolan Road.

The farmhands were back out in that field as we passed, putting up their hay.

We waved as we went by, and they waved back.

"That's it!" Mike cranked his bike around into a tight U-turn and headed back the way we'd just come.

We stopped and looked at each other.

"What's it?" Bits asked.

We followed Mike back to the fence along the hayfield. He left his bike in the ditch and climbed over the fence. Wading through hay stubble, he strode across the field toward the haying crew.

"Now what's all this?" Tiny dumped his bike and climbed the fence.

I was as curious as anyone else. When I struggled up over the fence, I tore my shirt on the strand of barbed wire along the top. I looked back and noticed that the girls were coming, too.

I had to lift my feet high to walk in the cut-off stubble. Extremely stiff and about eight inches tall, it crunched under my feet. Every now and then, a stem would throw me off when I stepped on it. And all the stubble that I didn't step on tried to trip me.

Mike was talking to a man in blue jeans and ball cap who was probably in charge.

The fellow turned to look at me, Tiny, and the girls. "So you guys need work, huh?"

That was news to me.

The man whipped out a cell phone and punched in some numbers. "Harry? Bring the other baler over right now. We might get this in yet." He slammed it shut. "You guys are lucky that it looks like rain."

He walked away.

Mike glowed. "We got jobs! All of us. And it's legal. Kids are allowed to work on a farm!"

Lynn wagged her head. "I don't understand. What's going on?"

Mike stepped in front of her. "You know how they make hay?"

"Not exactly. They cut grass and bale it."

"This isn't grass; it's alfalfa. But, yeah. They cut it with a mower. It lies in the sun and dries, then they come along with a tedding machine. That's a machine that flips it over so it dries on the other side. And makes it into long rows. Then the baler scoops up the rows, like here, and makes it into bales. If they're little bales like these, you store them in a barn. If they're the big roundish things, you leave them in the field."

Lynn shrugged. "I still don't get it."

Tiny explained, "If the hay gets rained on before they put it in the barn, it gets all moldy inside the bale. Spoils. It's ruined. So they have to make hay while the sun shines, see?"

Now Mike was jumping up and down, he was so excited. "They're bringing in another baler, and we're going to help them get the rest of the field put away before it rains. They need us, and we need them. Instant money, *compadres!*"

It didn't take me long to figure that one out. We would work only a couple hours at most. Either it would rain or the job would be finished. We had nothing to lose, and the farmer had everything to gain. So the Sugar Creek Gang was about to become a hay-making gang. Not bad.

Who knows? Maybe from the top of the hay wagon we'd have a better viewpoint, and we'd see some wolves.

10

The five of us, the gang, were lined up and waiting when the farmer brought his second hay baler into the field. I don't know much about farm machinery, but I know *old* when I see it. This baler was rusty, and it creaked. The tractor pulling it looked really ancient. It was a dull, faded green with rust and mud for trim. I knew nearly all new tractors have a cab to protect the driver. This one didn't. Behind the baler rattled an aged flatbed trailer the color of dry, gray wood.

The fellow who brought in the second rig must have been the farm owner. He pulled alongside and stared at us. He did not look happy.

The fellow in the ball cap stepped up beside us.

The farmer scowled. "I thought you said you got more help!"

The fellow in the cap shrugged. "They want to work. Do you want your hay in or not?"

"Bah!" The farmer scowled darker. "You kids ever work a baler before? Did you kids ever *see* a baler before?"

Mike nodded. "I can tell 'em what to do. We do fine. We work good. You'll see!"

The farmer slid down off his tractor. "Joe,

you run this rig. I'll take the other. You and you—" he pointed to Lynn and Tiny "—come with me." He strode over to the other tractor and sent a man from that crew to help us. The man introduced himself as Cal.

So it looked as if Bits and Mike and I would be working on the old, rickety equipment. Really old or brand-new didn't make any difference to me. I didn't have the foggiest idea what to do on any of it.

Joe's face looked a little as if he was regretting this. "OK. Who knows how to drive a tractor?"

And then Mike surprised us all by saying, "I do!" He clambered up to the tractor seat, but he didn't sit in it. He sort of stood in front of it, his feet resting on the pedals.

Joe said, "I don't quite think—"

But Mike was on his way. He arched his back against the seat, shoved one of the big pedals down, and hauled on a long lever with both hands. The tractor lurched and began to rumble forward. Mike was too short to see over the hood; he sort of leaned to one side and craned his neck out to see around it.

Joe wagged his head, grinning, and pointed to the far corner of the field. He yelled, "We'll start at that end!" and the Sugar Creek Gang was in business. Hay business.

That, my dear friends, is the grimiest, itchiest, hottest, dirtiest, dustiest, hardest business in the world.

As Mike explained, the tractor drove along

a ridge of dried hay that was raked into place by the tedding machine. The ridge of hay, called a windrow, traveled up a chute into the big, boxy baling machine. Clumsy arms and wheels and things clunked and whirred. The hay got mashed together inside and was pushed out the back as a solid, rectangular bale. These bundles weighed from eighty to a hundred pounds, Joe told me.

A conveyor sticking out the back of the baler dumped the bale out onto the flatbed trailer. There someone would scoop it up and stack it at the back. When the trailer was full, the tractor would haul it off to the barn.

Except for that someone who scoops up bales, it sounds like an automatic process, right? Wrong. Cal, the other hired man, did most of the bale stacking at the rear of the trailer. I dragged the bales back to him from the front of the trailer bed where they dropped off the baler. That's right; I was dragging a hundred pounds across that trailer floor, over and over and over.

Using a pitchfork (which, I was told, was not a pitchfork—it was a hayfork, and apparently there's a difference), Lynn walked along behind to rescue any hay that the baler missed. She flicked the wads of missed hay over onto the next windrow. The old baler missed a lot of hay.

Joe spent all his time unclogging the baler when it jammed up or wedged a bale in cockeyed. Usually he could keep things working while we rolled along. Sometimes, though, he'd yell to Mike to stop.

Then Mike would push on the brake pedal as hard as he could, and the tractor would jerk to a stop. Soon Joe would yell, and the tractor would lurch forward.

When the rig turned a corner, sometimes a bale would get pushed off the back, not onto the trailer but onto the ground. Joe would buck it back up on the trailer.

Hay is not soft. Especially not alfalfa. It's hard and scratchy. Alfalfa hay consists of stiff, dry stems with lots of dry little roundish leaves. The leaves and dust and hay bits swirl all around. They stick to your sweaty skin and work down behind your collar and inside your shirt. Your arms itch. All those dry, scratchy little pieces rub and burn.

I hate to admit this, but, more than anything else that day, I wanted a *bath*. I wanted to wash off the grit and dirt and hay that covered me. I got hot and cranky.

Bits and Tiny and even Lynn got grumpy. The only person who really loved what he was doing was Mike. He bounced around like a Labrador retriever playing fetch, always eager for more. Drove me nuts.

During a break while Joe hauled the filled trailer off to the barn, the farmer came over to us and said, "You kids are working out better than I thought you would. How about ten dollars instead of five?"

I thought, *How about a hundred dollars*

instead of ten? but I didn't say it. OK, so ten dollars wasn't much for all that work, but it was ten dollars more than we started out with that morning.

Toward the end, I noticed that, now and then, Mike would simply let the tractor drive itself and he'd climb down behind the seat to help Joe. So there the tractor would go in a straight line, nobody in the seat, no hand on the wheel. It would just keep chugging along at a little less than walking speed, all by itself. Amazing!

And then the accident happened. I don't know why I knew it was coming, but somehow I did.

As it turned the corner, the baler spit out a bale, and Joe walked over to get it. At the same time, the next bale in the conveyor wedged and stuck. Mike jumped down off the tractor right in front of the baler and darted to safety before the baler's wheels got to him.

I was going to yell at him, but, just that quick, he jumped up on the trailer tongue—the long wooden pole connecting the flatbed trailer to the back of the baler. The conveyor extended out directly over the tongue, so he grabbed onto the side of the conveyor, off balance.

"Mike, be careful!" was all I had time to shout.

Mike yelped. His arms flailed. His hands waved, trying desperately to find something to grab. His feet slipped. He was tipping off his perch! Falling!

The trailer wheels were sure to run right over him—flatten him. That trailer was half-loaded with tons of hay.

I couldn't think. All I could do was dive toward him, my arms stretched out straight forward. I grabbed.

I had his hair in one hand and his T-shirt in the other as I hit the deck of the trailer. Thumping down on my belly like that knocked most of the wind out of me. I couldn't move; I just hung on, with my chest on the deck and my arms hanging out in space. And I hung on. Hung on.

All Mike's weight was on my arms and chest. At the back of my mind, I knew he was still up off the ground, safe and away from the wheels.

The rig lurched to a stop.

Joe was yelling to me, but I couldn't let go. I was sobbing. I sort of realized that it was over, and Mike wasn't dead after all, but I couldn't let go of him. I don't know why. Joe and the farmer had to pry my fingers open.

And then I shifted from scared and relieved to embarrassed. Terribly embarrassed. Joe was saying something about a hero, but I sure wasn't one. Heroes don't cry when they do something heroic.

And I didn't have any way to blow my nose —no tissue or anything—and that was embarrassing, too.

Tiny was just plain furious. "We're outta here!" He grabbed Mike's arm. "No pay in the world is worth dying for, and Mike almost did just now. We're gone."

Mike started to protest, but he was crying, too. He didn't say anything. He stumbled a little and headed out across the hay stubble—the vast, clean, harvested field—toward the bikes.

A couple of big raindrops splattered against my arms.

The farmer came up then. "You kids saved my hay. We'll throw a tarp over this and take it in. Here. Here's a hundred. Split it up among you."

Lynn took it, solemnly agreeing that we would divide it evenly. We headed out across the long, empty field after Mike, as distant, rumbling thunder announced the rain.

11

Rain is cool. I mean, cool in all sorts of ways. We were really hot and sweaty and sticky, and the rain cooled us off as we rode along Nolan Road. It cooled us off emotionally too, I suppose. Tiny wasn't mad anymore, Mike wasn't crying, and I was back to normal—whatever normal is. And it was cool in the way it changed the whole mood of the world, gray and wet and yet hopeful. I don't know how to explain it.

We stopped at a little cowshed beside the road. It didn't smell like cows or manure anymore, and the grass around it grew long and green and tangled. Therefore, no cows. It surely had a door once, but not now. It yawned open, inviting us in.

So we rolled our bikes in to it to wait out the rain. Sitting in the shed doorway watching the rain made a welcome rest. A long, straight line of water running off the tin roof spattered by our feet. Big bubbles would appear along the row and then pop just that fast.

The hundred dollars that the farmer gave us was a fifty, a twenty, a ten, and four fives. It was probably everything he had in his wallet.

Lynn gave the twenty to Mike and the four fives to Tiny. "We'll have to break the fifty before we can divide the rest."

"It's way past lunch." I was really hungry. "Let's go back to town and eat at the Extra-burger."

Bits sniffed. "Not exactly way past. Twelve fifteen."

Lynn pulled the map out of her bike pack and opened it up. She pointed. "We're here. If we go north on this dirt road just ahead, we'll come out around Fifteenth, here. See?"

Tiny bobbed his head. "And there's an Extraburger at Fifteenth and Crestline."

So I wasn't the only one who was hungry.

The rain didn't last long. But since that little barn was comfortable and pleasant, we waited awhile for the leaves. When you're in a car, it doesn't matter. But when you're riding a bike, the trees that hang out over the roads are still dripping long after the rain quits. You might as well be in the rain. Finally the sky lightened, and we hit the trail again.

Tiny led the way onto that dirt road Lynn showed us. We passed a very old-fashioned-looking farm that had a two-story white house and a huge barn with two silos. All kinds of equipment stood about in the barnyard, and all of it was a lot newer than what we had spent the morning with.

I tried to imagine what it would be like to live on a farm like that and drive a tractor and milk cows and do all the stuff that goes along with it. My father grew up on a farm doing chores. He said I was missing a lot. Every time I had to mow the lawn, though, I didn't quite believe that.

And I imagined growing your own food. You raise a baby chicken or cow up to full-grown and then kill it and cook it. What a weird idea, until you think about it awhile.

According to the circle we drew on our map, we were pedaling right square up the middle of wolf country. Dr. Morgan at the museum had told us that wolves are usually nocturnal or crepuscular. *Crepuscular* is a fifty-dollar word meaning they get out and about in the very early morning or very late evening. Predawn and dusk. So we wouldn't expect to see wolves this time of day, midafternoon, even though the clouds made the day dark.

The next farm we passed was just the opposite of that big, prosperous one. This one had a tiny house that was probably all of two or three rooms. It needed painting. There were a couple of sheds and a chicken coop out back, also needing paint. A windmill that didn't turn stood in the side yard, and a rusty push mower had stalled out beside the white gravel driveway.

We were just about past the place when Lynn called, "Whoa!" She whipped around and pedaled back into that driveway. Of course we all followed her.

Beyond the house, a big blob of flowered-print cloth was squirming around at the base of the chicken shed. The shed's corners rested on blocks, putting it about a foot off the ground, and the fabric was mashed down against the gap.

Tiny wagged his head. "Now what?"

Lynn dumped her bike beside the chicken coop and anxiously asked the blob of fabric, "Ma'am, are you all right?"

A small, very old woman pulled her arm out from under the shed, rose to kneeling, and sat back on her heels. I'd never seen so many wrinkles in one place, but her face looked kind. "Now, who are you?" She wore a sunbonnet—a real, old-fashioned sunbonnet—made from the same cloth as her housedress.

"We were just passing by, and it looked like you were in trouble. Can we help?"

The lady studied us through scratched-up glasses. "Why, isn't that nice." She pointed under the coop. "I have to put up half a dozen chickens. I was going to have that chicken for dinner, but it got down under the coop, and I can't reach it."

Lynn dropped down to her knees. "Maybe I can. I'm smaller than you." She flopped down on her belly and stuck her face in the gap. "I see it. A white one?"

"Yes." The lady knelt down with one ear on the ground. She peered under. She sure was flexible for being so old.

Lynn squirmed and kicked and forced her body into the gap between the coop and the ground. When the gap had more than half swallowed her, she began to squirm back out.

Tiny and I grabbed her ankles and pulled. It speeded up the process a lot.

"Oh, my! Thank you, child!" the woman exclaimed. She sat back on her heels again.

Lynn reappeared, pretty grimy—but then we were all hay- and dirt-covered anyway. She was gripping a wad of bloodied white feathers. She gasped and threw it on the ground. "It doesn't have any head!"

The woman smiled. "No, dear, that's how you prepare a chicken to eat. You start by cutting off its head."

"But how . . ." Lynn looked again at that gap under the shed.

"Even after the head is gone, the body flops around awhile," the woman explained. "Didn't you ever hear 'running around like a chicken with its head cut off?'"

Lynn's eyes were hubcap size. "They actually *run* with no head?"

"All over. This one flopped under the coop."

So this old woman could start with a live chicken and come out with fried chicken or roast chicken or something. And then I got this brilliant flash of an idea. "Ma'am, you said you have to cut the heads off six of them and cook them?"

"Well, five of them I'll dress out and put in the freezer. Cook one."

"Ma'am, please, may I stay and help you and learn how to do it?" Boy, did that sound silly! So I tried to explain better. "You see, I'm going to be a great chef when I grow up, and I want to find out these things."

Bits giggled. "The first step is to turn on the oven, Les."

I shot her a dirty look.

The woman smiled. "So you're going to be a great chef." She got her feet under her and stood up. "Well, son, I'm not a great chef. I'm just an old widow who cooks plain food. But certainly you can stay and help, if you like."

"Thank you, ma'am! My name is Les Walker," and then I introduced everyone else.

Her name was Bertha Monroe, which tells you right there how old she was. How many people do *you* know named Bertha?

With the five of us following, she carried her headless chicken to a screened-in porch across the back of her house.

In a crate by the back door were her other five chickens, all with their heads on yet.

Tiny knelt beside it. "Miz Monroe, what happened to these chickens?"

"Dogs or something got into them. I heard a commotion, but I didn't see. These are the ones that got mauled. Best to butcher them right away before they start losing weight."

"Dogs." Tiny stood up, looking grim. "In the chicken yard?"

"Of course." The woman looked at him oddly.

"When?"

"Half an hour ago, I'd say." And then she reached into the crate for a chicken.

Tiny headed back out to the chicken yard, so I followed him.

"Think it's them?" I asked.

He studied the rain-wet dirt in the bare yard around the coop. "I know it's them." He pointed.

The damp soil was perfect for taking a footprint—not too dry and not too sloppy. Dog-like prints both huge and small mixed with chicken footprints all over the ground. Here and there you could see where a chicken's wing or tail had brushed briefly. If Mom were describing it, she'd say there'd been a melee—action all jumbled.

Tiny got down on his knees to stare at a nice set of tracks. "Look, Les. It's not just a couple wolves or coyotes or whatever. It's a family group. Big ones and little ones."

I could see it, too. I laid my hand, palm side down, on the largest print I saw. My hand didn't quite cover the print.

Tiny sat back on his heels and looked at me. "We had a sixty-pound dog once at the shelter, when the owner couldn't find a vet in town. He brought his dog out to us because Dr. Meyers was there. I thought that dog's feet were big."

"This one's bigger than sixty pounds? Is that what you're saying?"

"A lot bigger. This is getting ugly, Les."

12

I've never been able to figure out why I have the friends that I do. I mean this: You meet someone who is like you, and you two get along fine and do mostly the same stuff, but the friendship doesn't really click. And then you meet someone who's as different from you as horses from fleas, and that something clicks, and you're friends for life. Go figure.

Bertha Monroe was one of those friends-for-life people ten minutes after we met her. I can't explain why. She got along great with all five of us, in fact. She instantly became the whole Sugar Creek Gang's pal.

She was a real old-fashioned farm lady, too. She made jam and apple butter. She grew her own vegetables, canning some and freezing some. She raised chickens, a few beef cows, and a couple geese. She hung her washing out on long rope clotheslines propped up with poles. And, she said, once in a while she'd go down to a small pond at the back of her twenty acres and catch a few sunfish for dinner.

What a great life!

As Tiny and I went back to the house after looking at those tracks, Mrs. Monroe and Mike were dispatching yet another injured chicken. It didn't run without its head because the wolves had mangled its legs. But it flopped all over the ground awhile.

"Miz Monroe," Mike said, "when my mama kills a chicken, she hangs it upside down from the clothesline with its feet tied together. Then when she cuts its head off, it doesn't go anywhere." He reached into the crate for the last chicken, grabbing it expertly by a leg.

"So could I if my line was wire or plastic. But it's cotton rope, and the blood would soak into it. Then it would spot my clothes when I hung them." She picked up her hatchet. "You children had lunch?"

"Not yet, ma'am." Bits seemed fascinated by the dying chicken. "We were on our way to the Extraburger on Crestline."

"Afraid I can't make you the Super Deluxe Extraburger with curly fries, but I have fresh-baked bread and peanut butter and more strawberries than I can eat by myself. How about I hang these birds and then fix you a little something. We'll pluck them after lunch."

"Well, uh . . ." I hesitated.

So she showed us to the phone in her house, and we called our moms to get permission. Her phone was black and looked like something out of a 1950s movie. It had a dial. Dialing a phone is the slowest thing in the world. You turn the dial and wait for it to come back, and then you mess up the last number and have to start over.

And so we ate late lunch in the home of Bertha Monroe. I was right about the house.

Three rooms. It had a kitchen, a front room, and a bedroom. We gathered around a little kitchen table that only had three chairs, but Tiny sat on a box, and Mike simply stood there and seemed happy.

The homemade bread was even better than store-bought white bread, but I'd never tell my mom that. Mom thinks that if bread is pure white, it's lacking something.

Mrs. Monroe asked, "Lynn, are you feeling well? You've hardly touched your sandwich."

Lynn smiled, "And it's delicious, too. I guess I'm not very hungry."

Bits sniggered. "She's not used to blood and guts much. But if she hangs around us very long, she will be. Isn't that right, Tiny?"

And so Tiny explained about the rescue shelter where he volunteered. Mrs. Monroe asked all kinds of eager questions. Tiny did not mention the wolves or how crowded the shelter was because of them.

I noticed a set of dog dishes in the corner by the stove. So she had a dog. They were very heavy crockery; you don't find that much anymore. The name *TUFFY* was personalized on them. Was Tuffy the dog she had now, or did her present dog inherit those old dishes from some former dog? I didn't get a chance to ask because we were all talking about other stuff. And then I forgot to.

Lynn eventually did finish her lunch. I think it's because her parents taught her to eat what's served, not because she got her appetite back.

After lunch, we followed Mrs. Monroe out to her summer kitchen. This was a kind of shed separate from the house but attached to it with a sidewalk under a long roof. She called the walk "the breezeway." In the shed she kept canning jars, a big propane stove, and all sorts of giant tubs and pots.

"I make jam and can out here in summer," she said. "So that it doesn't heat the house up so bad."

She put a big pot of water on to boil, and we fetched in the chickens. They didn't move at all now, which suited me. We sat down around a big, round basket.

Mrs. Monroe dipped a chicken in the boiling water. To loosen the feathers, she said. Then she warned, "Let it cool a bit," and handed it to Mike. But he started right in, yanking out feathers by the handful.

We each got a dipped chicken. Man, was that fun! You grab a big wad of feathers and just pull them out. The wet feathers stick to your hands and arms so bad you can't let go of them. So here you are with these huge clumps of feathers at the ends of your arms. And then, naturally, your nose itches.

Tiny showed us how chickens (almost all birds, he said) are not covered all over with feathers. The feathers grow only in certain places, in patches, and the rest is bare. But the feathers in the patches fluff out to cover everything. Tiny even knew the correct words—*pterylae* for the feather areas and *apteria* for the bare spaces between. It's a poor day you don't learn something (but when I tried to tell Mom and Dad about it that night, I couldn't remember the words and had to look them up).

Mrs. Monroe took the last chicken for herself and still finished first. She grinned. "I've done a few of these."

I bet.

She turned on a gas burner and showed us how to singe the chickens. A lot of little pinfeathers, just tiny things, remain behind when you're done plucking a chicken. You burn them off carefully over an open flame.

She slit the chickens' bellies open with a sharp knife. She wouldn't let us do that. "Don't want your folks coming to me when you cut a finger off."

We all pulled the innards out of our chickens and separated out the heart, liver, and gizzard. She showed us how to cut the gizzard and turn it inside out to clean it.

And I'm proud to say that Lynn got up the nerve to do her own chicken. She didn't dive into the work nearly as eagerly as Mike did—or me—but she did it. And she finished it, even the gizzard part.

When we got done that afternoon, there were six dressed chickens just as if you'd bought them at the grocery store. Mrs. Monroe bagged up five of them for her freezer. She wrote the date on the bags.

"If you don't use them in a year," she said, "out they go."

Bits asked, "Do you throw much away?"

"Very little." She smiled. "But now and then I have a pretty strange menu for awhile, trying to use something up."

I heard a dog whine at the back screen door. The first thing I thought was, *Oh no! Her dog tangled with the wolves and got hurt!*

I glanced at Tiny, and it was obvious that he was thinking the same thing.

But no. The dog was fine. Mrs. Monroe walked over and let him in. "Tuffy"—that answered that question—"these are friends from Sugar Creek."

I liked that.

"How cute!" Lynn cooed. "His face is so sweet."

I got to admit it wasn't a bad dog as small dogs go. It stood maybe fifteen inches high. Pale brown, it was shaped and upholstered more or less like a mop. And talk about friendly! It squirmed around, licking us and being petted, and just getting acquainted in general.

Mrs. Monroe huffed. "Look at you, Tuffy! You've been playing down in the pond again."

The little pooch was all muddy and wet.

Mrs. Monroe warned, "Shove him away. Don't let him get you all dirty."

But you will recall we were already filthy from that haying. A little more dirt off a dog wasn't going to make a bit of difference.

And, sure, I petted him, too. I often wished we owned a dog, but I'd want a bigger one than this. It was curious—Dad called big dogs, especially big dogs of no particular breed, "farm dogs." Here was a dog on a working farm, and it was terrier size.

The chicken dressing was done. But just before we left, Mrs. Monroe showed me how she cut up a bird, and how she dredged it in seasoned flour and egg and milk. So I got another step closer to the goal of being a great chef.

On the bike ride home that afternoon, I thought a lot about Mrs. Monroe. There she lived, working hard every day, with a little brown dog as her only companion. She obviously wasn't making much money.

And I had never seen a happier, more contented person.

13

You can't buy a live chicken in this town.

I came to that conclusion when I looked for one to try out my new chef skills with.

Somehow, buying a chicken in a bag at the supermarket just wasn't the same thing. Mom suggested that if I wanted to try the flour-and-egg recipe Mrs. Monroe had shown me, I could slice up and fry an eggplant. That is absolutely not the same thing. I couldn't tell if she was teasing me or not. Probably, she was.

All this talking took place at breakfast the morning after our adventures in hay and feathers. Mom said I could make supper that night. So I decided to buy a chicken and wow them all.

I called up Bits to see if she wanted to go grocery shopping and also get some ice cream. No, she said, she was busy. I know what she was busy at. Computer games.

I called up Lynn and got their answering machine.

I called up Tiny, but he was volunteering at the shelter.

I called up Mike. His mom said he was out helping his brothers. Apparently they'd promised him a raise.

It was starting to look like a long, long day.

Ice cream doesn't taste half so good when you eat it alone.

Since it would be hours and hours before I'd even think about starting to cook dinner, I killed some time by riding out to Nolan Road again. The ground was still a little damp from that rain yesterday. Maybe, I thought, I could find some more wolf tracks.

And now you're thinking, *Why not just buy a chicken from Mrs. Monroe?*

I thought of it. But then I remembered something she mentioned yesterday. Losing six hens was putting her short; she was afraid she would no longer get enough eggs. It seems she sold eggs to some regular customers—people who bought from her because they wanted eggs from free-range chickens. And now some of her best layers were lying naked in her freezer. She needed every hen. So I wasn't even going to ask.

The bank thermometer by Crestline Plaza said 83, but it felt a lot hotter than that. I guess that was because of the moisture in the air left over from yesterday's rain. The humidity. When it's humid, warm feels warmer.

I took 22d Street south. At Cedar, the pavement ended. It was still several miles to that dirt road that went past Mrs. Monroe's place.

And there, trotting along the roadside, came Tuffy!

I dropped my bike and sat down beside it. "Hey, Tuffy! Come here, old top! Come to me."

Tuffy didn't remember me at first. He growled and backed away, his white teeth bared.

"Oh, come on, Tuffy. It's me."

He thought about it, I guess, because after a moment or two he came trotting over and squirmed against me, licking. His wiggly little body felt very warm beneath that silky brown fur.

"You're not going away from your home, and you're not going toward it. What's the matter, fella? Lost?"

Squirm, squirm, squirm. Lick, lick, lick.

He wasn't wearing a collar. I suppose dogs that stay on the farm wouldn't need one. But if someone else found Tuffy, how would he or she know whose dog this was?

"Oh, wow!" One of his floppy little ears was torn, and the injury was fresh too. In fact, blood was drying into his coat in a couple places. "So you got into a fight. I don't think getting hit by a car would do this. Well, come on, Tuffy. Let's take you home."

Tuffy wasn't very heavy. Once I straddled my bike, I scooped him up and cradled him in my left arm. That kept the right hand free for steering, shifting gears, and braking. OK, so it wasn't the safest way to ride a bike, but it wasn't the most dangerous, either. And I didn't have a rope or leash or anything to walk him with.

Tuffy didn't like going anywhere that way. But I held him tight, and pretty soon he resigned himself to being hauled home.

When I got there, Mrs. Monroe was sitting on her front porch shelling peas. "Well, hello, Les! And *Tuffy*. Now what?" She was wearing a different housedress—this one had stripes instead of flowers. No sunbonnet, but, of course, she was under the porch roof.

"Hello, Mrs. Monroe. I found him out on the road and was afraid he was lost." I dumped my bike and carried the dog up onto the porch. "He tore an ear." I showed her.

She wagged her head. "That dog. His mother was the same way. Always getting into something." She gathered her little pooch into her lap to get a better look at the ear.

"Do you ever tie him up, ma'am?"

"Oh, no. Gracious, no. He doesn't go far. Just up to the corner of Lindsey."

"But I found him clear up by where the pavement starts."

"Oh my. Maybe he did get lost. Chasing a rabbit or something, forgot where he was." She smiled. "He never manages to catch anything. And he doesn't chase the chickens, or he'd be out of here in a flash."

A big brown delivery truck came rumbling down the gravel road. It managed to raise some dust in spite of the dampness. The driver, a blonde woman, stopped in front of Mrs. Monroe's house. She looked at one of those little computer boxes that you sign with an electronic stylus, and then at the numbers on Mrs. Monroe's mailbox. She frowned.

She disappeared into the back of her truck. Moments later, she came out with a big brown box sort of like a deep-dish pizza box. Little round holes ventilated all four sides.

And it peeped. I mean, the whole box peeped. In fact, it peeped very loudly, sort of one long, continuous chirp.

She stepped up to the porch. "Bertha Monroe?"

"I can't believe it. My chicks arrived already! I only phoned in the order yesterday afternoon." Mrs. Monroe set her bowls of shelled and unshelled peas aside and stood up.

"Mail order chickens?" I gaped. "Alive?"

"The world is happening much too fast these days, Les. It used to take a month to order and receive chickens."

The driver handed Mrs. Monroe the sign-in box and smiled. "My truck has been sounding like the inside of an aviary all morning. Those little 'leather lungs' make a lot of noise."

Mrs. Monroe signed for her loud parcel. "Les, I'm glad you came. I can use a little help setting up the brooder. I think it's up in the top of the barn."

And do you know what we did? Pretty much forgot about Tuffy, that's what we did.

I climbed up into the haymow of her little barn and handed a shallow sheet metal cone down to her. She also wanted some cartons full of metal brooder pieces. We put it all together on the floor of the chicken house.

What we had when we were done looked like something from a *Star Wars* movie. The shallow cone was a roof, which we suspended from the top rafter by a chain. The wide part down, it hung a foot or so off the floor. It had a light bulb up inside it so that the area under the cone was very brightly lighted. The bulb was more for heat than light, Mrs. Monroe explained.

We put up a little portable fence to keep the chicks confined to the area under the roof. We set up a long, narrow feed trough and a watering device. We scattered sawdust and chick feed. Then she turned her babies out into their new home.

"Half are barred Plymouth Rocks and half are buff Orpingtons." Mrs. Monroe put the emptied box aside. "I get chickens that lay brown eggs because the brown eggs sell better."

"They all look alike to me. Fluffy little yellow chicks."

"You'll be able to tell them apart once they start getting feathers."

So we were finished. "I really enjoyed this, Mrs. Monroe. Thank you for letting me help."

"Why, thank you for helping! Can you stay for lunch?"

"I better not. Thank you for asking me. I have things I gotta do at home."

One of them was cooking a chicken. But I didn't mention that. I headed back for my bike. Then I stopped. "Is Tuffy around?"

"Gone again." Mrs. Monroe shook her head. "Silly dog."

I didn't want to scare her. On the other hand, I had seen the full house at the rescue shelter. I knew what those wolves or whatever could do.

I licked my lips. "Uh, ma'am? I don't know if you heard, but coyotes or something have been causing trouble around here lately. Some say it's wolves. Whatever, Tuffy's awfully small. He could get hurt or killed if the pack finds him."

"Mm." She frowned. "I did hear something about it, but I didn't realize it was around here. You're probably right. I should keep him closer to home. I'd better keep his collar on him, too. It has my phone number on it."

"Yeah, that would be good. It was lucky I happened to know him. A stranger wouldn't have. Well, g'bye."

"Good-bye. And thank you again, Les."

I didn't say any more, but that comment about a collar sounded as if she was not going to keep him tied. Tuffy was her dog, not mine. It was none of my business whether she let him go out roaming. Still, I worried. He was so little.

As I got on my bike and started pedaling back toward town, I heard her say again, "Silly little dog."

14

Now in case you are wondering what happened to that cold turkey that was my first attempt as a chef, we managed to make room for it in the fridge. We roasted it the next day. But the Sugar Creek Gang wasn't there the next night to help eat it, so we had an awful lot of turkey left over.

Still do.

Probably always will. The thing is endless.

Mom showed me how to freeze meat—the turkey, specifically—to keep it fresh. Now over a week later, I went back into the freezer and labeled all the packages of frozen turkey with the date.

"That," I explained importantly to Mom, "is so we know to use it before it dries out or goes bad."

She wasn't as impressed as I thought she'd be.

She wasn't impressed when I cut up the whole fryer I bought, either. She and Mrs. Monroe didn't cut up a chicken in exactly the same way. When I suggested that Mrs. Monroe did it the "right" way, things got pretty cool in the kitchen. So I just shut up about Mrs. Monroe.

You'll recall that Mrs. Monroe did all the knife work when we helped at her house. Now I got to do my own cutting. It's not nearly as easy as it looks when someone else is doing it. Not nearly. Mom showed me how to break the joints backward so I wouldn't cut my fingers off.

For a few cents a pound more, you can get your chicken already cut up. Next time, I decided, I might consider that.

It took me a little longer to put the meal together than I intended, and we ended up eating past 7:30 that night. That didn't go over real well, either. The chicken was OK but not nearly as good as Mom's, the potatoes weren't quite done, and the peas turned out mushy. I don't know how that happened. I'd put salads together at four o'clock, so they looked a little wilted by the time we sat down.

To top it off, it was my week to do the dishes. I didn't realize how many pots and pans I'd used until I had to wash them.

I finished in the kitchen well after 9:00. I was pooped, discouraged, and confused. Other than that, I was just fine, thank you.

The overhead light was on in the garage, and loud noise came from there. So I went out to see what Dad was doing.

He was making something. Every now and then he'd get this urge to use the expensive woodworking tools Mom and his folks gave him from time to time. Tonight he was doing unspeakable things to a couple of pressure-treated one-by-fours.

I waited until the radial arm saw stopped. "What's all this gonna be?"

"Adirondack chairs."

"We don't live anywhere near the Adirondacks."

"You don't live anywhere near Paris, but you eat french fries."

Well, you can't beat that logic with a stick. I watched him cut some angled boards. It's a firm rule at our house: If someone is using power tools, no talking. No distraction. That even includes using the lawn mower.

When the saw stopped again, I asked, "Dad? Do you suppose God is telling me I'm probably not gonna be a great chef?"

"Maybe. Or maybe He's just telling you that you need practice."

So not only did you have to figure out where and how God was speaking to you, you had to figure out what He was saying too. This was getting very complicated.

Before I had time to think much about that new twist, Dad asked, "How long does it take your mom to make dinner?"

"Hour or so. Give or take."

"How long has she been doing it?"

I shrugged. "Forever. Since she got married. I dunno."

"We had hot dogs three times a week when we first married. And half raw chicken a few times. Skill comes with doing it awhile." He set his band saw table at a twenty-degree angle and locked the gate in place.

I remembered when my grandparents gave him that saw. It took him hours, with the instruction manual propped nearby, to figure out how to do things with it. Now he could make all sorts of weird shapes without even thinking about it.

He asked, "How long did it take you to learn to rollerblade?"

Now that was a touchy subject. I broke an arm rollerblading. "Not quite long enough."

He laughed. "Get my point?"

"Yes, sir. But I still don't know what God is saying or how He's saying it."

"You will, Son. Isn't it about bedtime?"

"Yeah, I guess. G'night."

"Good night."

So I headed back into the house, wondering about God speaking and also wondering what an Adirondack chair was. As I passed the family room I heard Catherine whining, "But, Mommy, it's summer vacation! Just a little while?" So I knew the girls were trying to renegotiate bedtime.

Not me. I was going to fall asleep so fast, I wouldn't even hear the pillow crumple. But I sure wasn't going to admit that to Mom or Dad.

I good-nighted everyone and dragged my weary body up the stairs. The phone rang when I was halfway up, but I'd let one of the negotiators answer it.

I was halfway through the bathroom door when Mom called, "Les? It's for you."

Me? At almost ten o'clock at night? I picked up the phone in Mom and Dad's bedroom. "Hello?"

Bits growled, "I sent you an e-mail. Why didn't you answer?"

"Huh?" Then my brain connected back up. "Well, two reasons. One is, I was busy and didn't pull my mail down today. The other is, I've adopted my father's policy about e-mail."

"What's that?" she snarled accusingly. "Ignore it?"

"A long time ago, he got mad when people would expect him to do something instantly just because they sent him an e-mail note. He said, 'Other people's mail does not instantly obligate me.' And you don't know how long it took me to learn to say all that fast. Anyway, his policy is, when you get to it, you get to it."

"Thank you for sharing that, but it's more than I wanted to know."

"You asked what his policy was. If you don't like the answer, don't ask the question."

OK, so I was being crabby with her. And I knew I shouldn't, even though she was crabby at me. But I was tired and not in a good mood. That's not an excuse, understand. But it's the reason.

She didn't sound any less cranky. "I don't know why I bother with you. But I need you tomorrow. Daddy has to be in court, and he's taking me with him. I'm not allowed to take anything but books or paper and crayons. I don't want to go alone. He said you could come."

"You mean spend the whole day in the courthouse? I always said you were a bad customer, Bits, but I didn't think you were that bad."

"Hah, hah." But then her tone of voice changed from cranky to pleading. Even scared. "Come with me, will you, Les?"

"Sure." If I had to do something like that, I'd be scared, too—scared of being bored to death. "I'll come."

15

So the next morning, Bits's dad took us to the courthouse.

You don't know *boring* until you sit six hours in a courthouse. If we got to watch a murder trial, I bet it wouldn't be boring. But we had to stay in this little room near the room where people come to get selected for juries. We weren't supposed to talk to any of those people. No TV set. Not even a phone. Just Bits and me and a pad of paper and crayons.

We played hangman. That lasted about forty minutes. Five hours and twenty minutes to go. We drew pictures. Another half hour gone. Tick-tack-toe: ten minutes.

On a shelf I found a long telephone extension cord with a jack at each end. "Bits? Do you suppose your dad had the phone taken out?"

"Wouldn't put it past him." Her mood had not improved a millimeter.

I tied the ends together as best I could and set it up among my fingers for a cat's-cradle game. So for an hour or so we passed the cat's cradle back and forth. One time, we didn't lose it until the tenth pass. She showed me how to make Witch's Broom, and I showed her Magic Diamond. By then, our fingers were so tired from working that bulky phone cord that we quit.

She sprawled back in a chair that was too big for her and put her feet up on the table. "You're not near as much fun to be with as I thought."

"You're no vacation at the beach, either. Why's your dad doing this?"

"Because he hates me, and he's torturing me."

"Yeah, sure. You know, sometimes I make a lousy decision, but this one was one of the lousiest—agreeing to come along with you. He gets to torture both of us."

And from behind me came her dad's voice. "Ready for lunch, you two?"

I sure was. I jumped up.

Sergeant Ware looked really fine in his full police officer's uniform. He stood in the doorway a moment studying us oddly. He frowned at the tangled, kinked telephone cord on the table. "This isn't working, is it? Well, let's go eat."

We walked down to the Dog House on Le-Grande without saying much. I ordered two footlongs. Bits fussed over the overhead menu awhile and picked chicken nuggets. Her dad got a burger and fries. I snatched a couple napkins each (they were small), the catsup, straws, and relish. Bits went off to claim a table.

When we settled in with lunch, we still hadn't said much except for Bits. She dipped her nuggets in catsup while she complained because she hadn't ordered hot dogs.

We were nearly done when her dad said, "If

I drop you two off at Sugar Creek Park, will you stay there until I take you home later this afternoon?"

"Yes, sir!" I was ready for that.

"Daddy, can't you just take us home?" Bits whined.

I looked at her. "I thought you liked the park. That's where I first met you."

"Daa-deee?"

"It's the park or the courthouse, Bits. Either way, you stay where you're put." Her father sounded put out.

She didn't say anything, so I won the vote by her abstention.

Sergeant Ware drove us to the park and dropped us off in the picnic area parking lot. "I'll pick you up as soon as court lets out. Remember what I said: you two stay together." And away he went.

I gestured toward the trailhead. "Where do you want to go? Want to go see if the big painted turtle's hanging out? It's usually sunning this time of day."

"I don't care. I don't want to go anywhere." She kicked a loose stone out across the asphalt.

"Hey, look!" I pointed. "Here come Mike and Tiny!"

The two of them rolled up to us on their bikes. I walked over to the rack with them as they locked up.

Tiny asked, "Where's your bikes?"

"We buried them. What are you doing here?"

"Just thought we'd come see what's happening. Lynn's coming, too. Don't you read your e-mail?"

"He prefers to ignore it." Bits sounded really sarcastic.

"Let's wait till Lynn gets here and then find that big turtle." Tiny ambled over to the nearest picnic table, all elbows and long strides. He sat on it the way he usually did—sitting on the table part with his feet on the seat.

He grabbed the binoculars around his neck and whipped them up to peer at bushes. "Goldfinch."

I twisted around just in time to see a blur of black and lemon yellow flit from the grass into the brush.

Mike was bubbling, but then, Mike usually bubbled. "Hey, Les! I made ten dollars this morning!"

"That's great." He made ten dollars while I sat around all morning in the courthouse in a vacant room with a crabby girl. For that I got lunch.

Mike went on. "I helped out my brothers, and they gave me some money. And then Mrs. Muñoz across the street needed some trash hauled to the curb, so I did it, and she gave me a dollar. A dollar for five minutes of work! That's twelve dollars an hour!"

Bits scowled. "Mike, all you ever talk about is making more money. Money, money, money! You're obsessed with it."

"Am not!"

"Are too! Look at you! You were more than willing to break the law and work in a grooming parlor where you're not legally allowed to. You take big chances just to make a few bucks. I mean big—on that farm, you almost got yourself killed on machinery that's too big for you. You're obsessive, all right. You're nuts."

And Mike exploded. "Who you calling nuts? *You're* the one plays them computer games all day long. Don't even stop to breathe. You're the obsessed one!"

"Am not!"

"You're the one is addicted, girl!" Mike was yelling now. "Addicted like my uncle is to booze and my cousin Raphael is to gambling. You do it all day. Can't stop."

"I can quit anytime I want to!"

Mike laughed. "You mean anytime your papa makes you."

Tiny roared, "Cut it out, you two! Quit slashing at each other."

"Tell *him* to cut it out!" Bits barked.

"Hey, come on, Bits." I held my hands up. "He's right. Lynn's worried about you. She thinks you got a problem. And I know for a fact your dad thinks so. That's why he made you come with him today, right?"

Well, as soon as that came out of my mouth, I knew it was the wrong thing to say.

So I tried to patch it up. "I mean, you're both right, you know. And both wrong. Mike, you do have a money problem, and, Bits, you do have a game problem. Leave it at that. Just quit fighting, both of you. You guys are supposed to be Sugar Creekers."

Mike and Bits blew up at me in unison, yelling and accusing me of being wrong and nasty.

Then here came Lynn on her bike. If anyone could calm the whole scene down, it was Lynn.

On the other hand, an awful lot of hurtful things were already flying around. I just hoped she wasn't too late.

16

Lynn pulled in beside us, and I know she didn't realize until just then that she was rolling into the middle of an argument. She looked confused. "What's going on?"

"'Blessed are the peacemakers,' Lynn," I said. "You're about to be blessed. At least, I hope you are."

Bits pointed hand and arm at Lynn. "You stay out of this, Little Miss Perfect!"

Lynn mouthed, *Perfect?* as she stood there. Then her mouth silently sagged open.

"Hey, come on, you guys . . ." I begged.

Tiny was a little more direct. "Quit this, all of you, or I'm leaving."

"You stay out of this, too!" Bits hollered at Tiny.

"What is this?" Lynn looked more confused.

I'm sure Mike sensed an ally, or maybe he remembered that I had just mentioned Lynn's fears about Bits. "Here, Lynn will tell you. You got a big problem, Bits. Lynn knows it. She said so."

"Oh, she did! Since when was it any of your business, Miss Perfect?"

"*What?* Now stop it, and please tell me what's going on." Lynn glanced from face to face. "I thought we were here to go look for the turtle."

"Mike's here to straighten out the whole world all except himself," Bits sneered.

"I am not!" Mike wailed.

Lynn still hadn't lost her calm. I don't know how she did it. "I'm sure it's something you can talk out. Why can't you—"

"Oh, stuff it!" Bits yelled.

"Stop it, you two!" Tiny raised a hand.

Then Mike started yelling at Lynn too, and that surprised me. "Just cause my pop ain't no zippy-do professor like your pop is, don't mean nothing! We ain't poor!"

Quietly Lynn purred, "Nobody said you were."

"Everybody says that! We're on so many charity lists, you don't believe how many. We got four turkeys last Thanksgiving. And three food baskets at Christmas with turkeys in them!"

"That's a lot of turkeys." I remembered how many leftovers we still had in our freezer from just one.

Mike was still rolling. "But when my pop got laid off and we couldn't pay the light bill unless we went hungry, where were all them fine charities? You charity people, you give stuff to poor people on holidays so you'll feel good. It don't have nothing to do with helping people who need help."

"But—"

"And I ain't never gonna be a charity case, understand? Never!" Mike was so revved up he had tears in his eyes.

Bits hadn't mellowed in the slightest. "You don't know the first thing about charity giving! Sometimes people give just 'cause they care. People who give help don't have to, you know. Besides, you don't have to blame us for what grown-ups do! And it doesn't change anything, anyway. You're still a money addict!"

Tiny leaped off the picnic table. "I get enough fighting at home. I don't need this." He marched toward his bike.

"Hey, come on! All of you!" I yelled, but no one listened to me.

Bits and Mike were arguing back and forth about who was the worse addict.

Lynn wagged her head. "I can't believe you two. Why can't you just—"

Mike turned on her. "Let's see you apply for food stamps, and then you can say what we ought to do!"

Lynn looked hurt.

Mike brushed past her and headed for his bike.

If Lynn broke into tears—and she looked ready to—none of us knew about it. Tiny was gone, Mike was going, and now she got on her bike and just rode away.

I'd promised Bits's dad I would stay with her all afternoon and that we'd both stay in the park.

It was going to be a long, long afternoon— longer even than the morning had been.

Forget about being a great chef. I'd make better money as a lawyer.

17

You could safely say the day was a fizzle. Make that two days. My less-than-stellar performance cooking chicken the day before still bummed me out. And then Mike and Bits blew up. And Lynn went home hurt and sad. And Tiny went home angry. And Bits and I sort of pouted together but apart all afternoon, our backs to each other most of the time. For hours, until her dad got there.

We climbed into his car without saying anything. He pulled into their driveway, I thanked him for lunch, got out, said good-bye, and walked across the street to my own house.

Hannah greeted me as only Hannah can: "Mommy wants you to take the garbage out. And a friend of Daddy's will be coming for dinner, so get a shower and wash your hair. You look like you were dragged through a swamp."

"I was not dragged through a swamp! I went through it voluntarily."

And I *had* gone voluntarily. Bits and I found that big painted turtle a couple hundred yards back in the swamp trail, where it usually basked. It was the only positive thing we did all day.

Dinner tasted good because this time Mom cooked it. Dad took his friend, a fellow he went to law school with, to the airport. I did the dishes.

I went upstairs to my room to read. But I couldn't concentrate, so I gave that up. I tried to work on my half-finished airplane model (an F-16 fighter, if you're wondering which one). Even that wasn't interesting.

I imagined what it would be like to live on a farm. Hard work. That part I could see. But it would be fun too, with a lot of open space to run around in. Maybe we'd have a farm pond like Mrs. Monroe's and stock it with catfish and crappies.

Mostly, though, I just sprawled out in my chair by my little dormer window. I was all jumbled up inside. Mike was as much of it as anything. Poor old Mike, so angry at the world.

It was getting dusk now. The light from Dad's headlights flowed across the barberry hedge. I heard the garage door grind open and shut. I went downstairs past the family room, where the TV was blaring, and into Dad's den.

He was just sitting down with the newspaper. "Isn't it about bedtime?"

"Yeah, about."

So I flopped down in the chair beside his and tried to tell him a little of how Mike felt. I didn't bother with the gang's blowup. That was too complicated to describe. I didn't get Mike's story across very well, either, I thought.

Or maybe I did, because Dad put aside his paper and sat back in his recliner with his eyes closed. Some might think he was falling asleep, but I knew better. He was thinking. He had just turned his full attention to the inside of his head.

A few minutes later he sat bolt upright and, reaching mightily, pulled his computer keyboard off the desk behind him. He settled it into his lap and hit a couple of keys without looking at the monitor.

I craned my neck to see over the back of my chair. The screen saver disappeared, and his writing program popped up.

"OK, Les, can you tell me verbatim what he said?"

"Word for word, you mean?"

He nodded. "As much as you can."

"I don't know. It's a stretch." So I sat back, too, and stared at the ceiling. I managed to dredge up most of the bits and pieces but not in the right order. Dad said the order didn't matter. He was copying down what I remembered, typing wildly.

When I'd about got it all, I asked, "What are you going to do with that? I don't want to embarrass Mike."

"I'm not sure what I'll do with it yet." Dad smiled. "But we won't embarrass him. I promise. Go to bed."

"OK. Good night." And I headed back upstairs.

I didn't go right to bed, though. I was still too churned up inside. I turned out my light and sat in the dark by the window to watch the moon come up. It was just past full, a wee bit lopsided but still very bright.

The window didn't have a screen—Dad said he was going to get to that one of these days—but I opened the window wide anyway, clear open. The fresh, cool air of night came floating in.

The sky was light gray from all the city lights. The rising moon washed it grayer and lighter. Now I could see the moon peeking out beyond the Herrons' rooftop. Then Herrons' old TV antenna, still attached to the chimney years after they went to cable, cut the moon in two with a long black line.

I didn't know what to do. Everything weighed so heavy. It wasn't *heavy* heavy, like someone getting very sick or dying. Just sort of heavy. An annoying heavy. You feel unbalanced. Unsettled. At loose ends. The world isn't quite right. Know what I mean?

Every night when I was a little kid, Mom would sit on the bed while I got down on my knees and said my prayers. I didn't really know who I was talking to then. I was just a little kid. So I said those prayers and ended them by blessing everything, including the cat we had at the time.

I was older now and on my own at prayer time. I was sure Mom and Dad expected me to be praying by myself. I hadn't been.

The moon rose above the chimney and nearly got blotted out by Herrons' maple. Just above the tree, the power lines waited, ready to cut it in half crossways.

Where do you start? Those prayers I rattled off when I was little didn't seem like the right stuff anymore, what with me going on twelve now.

Besides, I wasn't exactly on easy speaking terms with God and couldn't tell if I ever had been. That was discouraging in itself.

I didn't get on my knees. I didn't even close my eyes. I watched the world out there change, feeling its cool breath come in the open window.

Mom always said you begin with thanks and praise, whatever the prayer. She said God more than anyone else in the universe deserves it.

I thank You for thinking up the gift of Your Son Jesus. For letting Him pay for all the messing up I do. You didn't have to do that, and I'm thankful You did. Especially since I can't begin to pay for all these messes by myself.

I didn't know how to frame the next part in prayer language—you know, the fancy words preachers use sometimes when they really get wound up. Finally, I decided I probably didn't have to.

You know what I've been thinking, because You know all our thoughts. The Bible says so.

The gang just exploded. I don't know what to do or how to help it get back together. I don't know how to find out what Your will is. I want to, I really do. I just don't know how. Please help me. Help us.

The moon finally coasted clear of the maple, the wires, and the power transformer.

I didn't ask God for anything more. I'd already asked for plenty, I figured. I just kind of waited. It was the first time I'd prayed without quitting as soon as I'd listed what I wanted. I guess you could say I stopped to listen.

So here I sat in this chair, not on my knees

with my face mashed into the bedspread the way I used to. I was watching God's moon and the interesting things it did with its light. How black the shadows were. How silver the lighted areas. How different it was from the sun—or from stars, for that matter. How it pulled itself free of the antenna and tree and power lines and soared triumphant over everything.

The moon seemed to slow down and just hang there. It filled our yard with soft, gray light.

Did God speak to me then? I don't know. I heard no voice or anything. I didn't get this strong notion that I must go out and march around the city seven times blowing trumpets or something. Nothing like that.

But pretty soon, things didn't weigh so heavy anymore. That off balance feeling quietly went away. If God wanted me to do something, He'd let me know. He wouldn't ignore me. I could depend on that. Sure, I'd keep trying to think out His will, but He'd help. I just knew it.

I'd keep asking Him to give Mike and Bits comfort, and He would. The problems among the kids would work out. Maybe I'd have a hand, with God's help, in healing the split. Maybe. Maybe I'd even learn how to cook chicken.

I was talking to God, and He was talking to me, and no words were passing back and forth. Sure, God could do that—He can do anything! —but I never before knew that I could. It was the most amazing thing.

Whatever happened, the moon—God's moon—would rise tomorrow and the next night and the next. The sun would come up on schedule. I wasn't in control of any of that, but He was. I couldn't control anything at all. But He could.

The world was all right.

18

The next morning at breakfast, I was going to tell Mom and Dad about my prayer time last night, but I didn't know how to describe it. It was still amazing me, but it wasn't something solid you could talk about. I wasn't even sure I could describe it in words. Then Dad mentioned that the grass was getting pretty long again. Nothing kills a vague spiritual happening like a megadose of reality.

So after breakfast, Dad went to work, Mom went into the den to write, Hannah and Catherine went off to the neighbor's, and I headed for the shed.

The grass was green and juicy and still a little wet. It kept wadding up under the mower and choking the hole where it was supposed to blow into the catcher. What I'm saying is, it took me a long time to do a fairly short job. I did up the trees and flower bed edges with the trimmer.

And yes, I knew you never ever let the fishline in a trimmer touch tree bark. Never. Sooner or later, a fishline trimmer will chew all the way through the bark of most any tree. Then it cuts off the tree's tiny little pipes—the cambium— that the tree uses to draw water and food up from the roots. If the tree can't get water and nutrients anymore, it shrivels up, and there's nothing you can do to save it.

You're hearing the voice of experience. I accidentally girdled a couple trees in Seattle, and they died.

Mom said, "Les, you're a great chef. How about making lunch? I'm in the middle of things here."

All great chefs started at the bottom, I was sure, so I guessed I would, too. I got out some of that cooked and frozen turkey, the bread, lettuce, mayo, and all, and a can of soup.

The soup was an easy hit. I just followed the directions on the label. The label even said what size pan to use. Medium.

The turkey I thawed in the microwave. It was still cold, but no ice. It took me awhile to build the sandwiches. It's a slower process than you'd think.

I set out the dishes and flatware, poured iced tea, swiped the vase of flowers out of the living room and put it on the kitchen table, and found napkins. When I yelled, "Lunch is ready," the table looked pretty good.

Mom seemed surprised. She sat down and lifted her bread slice to peek under. "Why, Les, this is excellent!"

We said grace. No sooner was the "amen" spoken than the phone rang.

Mom sighed. "Mealtime. It never fails."

I picked up the phone on the kitchen counter. "Walker residence. Oh, hi, Dad. Here's Mom."

But he said, "It's you I'm calling, Les."

"Why me?"

"Remind your mom that the church board meeting is tonight. I'll pick you up as soon as I'm done here. We'll grab a burger and go to the meeting."

"We? You mean both of us?"

"Yes. You too."

I was about to turn down the invitation—I mean, how boring can you get?—but then I decided he must be doing this for some good reason. "OK."

"So tell your mom we won't need dinner tonight."

"Wouldn't you know it. Here I finally become a great chef, and you don't need me anymore. OK, I'll tell her."

So there I was seven hours later, sitting in a church board meeting. Dad was not a board member, but he gave them free legal advice as a gift to the church. He was in on nearly all the meetings. I felt very out of place among that bunch of business folk.

And I'm here to tell you it was every bit as boring as I feared. More, even.

Until they got to "new business."

Dad said, "I have some. A young friend revealed to Les here some of his thoughts about charity. They are things we as Christians must know." He brought a sheaf of papers out of his briefcase and handed them around to everyone. He even gave me a copy.

He looked at the secretary. "I request that this be entered into the minutes."

He had written down Mike's complaint pretty much word for word. I followed along as he read it out loud to the board. It reminded me all over again about Mike's frustration and anger.

The room was awfully quiet. Dad laid the paper aside. "This boy is absolutely right. We appear to give to the needy seasonally in order to feel good. His feelings are extremely intense. They should be. And now mine are as well."

I couldn't believe it! This was amazing.

Dad continued, "I will work out with you how you want the mission statement worded, but I will pester and push until we act on this. No more seasonal giving unless it is an extension of a program already in place. We are called to help people when they have need, not just when it feels good to us."

The pastor asked, "What are you suggesting? We already have a food basket program . . ."

"Perhaps have a closet full of nonperishable items—so people in need can come anytime, without being looked down upon. The church secretary could handle distribution to people who come during office hours. We can set up deals with local merchants, so the church can obtain at cost the things people in need might have to have. Simple things, often. Shoes. Personal necessities."

Boy, was I glad I came!

Dad ended with, "This boy has hit on the head the problem with the charity program in most churches. I'm not throwing rocks at us. Most churches. We never hear from the other side, so we think we're doing just fine. We have to do better than that. Jesus expected it."

What Dad did not mention was that our old church up in Seattle already did what he was talking about. They delivered bags of groceries to people who needed them, fed the church members who were poor—did their thing day by day. In fact, now that I thought about it, they didn't do anything extra on holidays except throw big "everybody come" feasts. At the holiday feeds, people with lots of money and people with none sat together around the tables.

The pastor frowned. "It will be hard to sell the congregation on a change. I'm sure most of them will say we're already fulfilling our obligation to the needy."

Dad sat back smiling. "Like I said, this is very important to me. We can surely get something going."

And I knew from the way he said it that, yes, they would get something going.

That night I sat down in my chair again and opened the window wide. Whether the gang's blowup got healed was important to me. Sure. But even if that never happened, Mike's part of it had led to great things to be done to help many people. That really impressed me. I thought for a while about how God turned those few minutes when Mike spilled out his anger into something good.

I went to bed before the moon came up, because, as you know, it rises later every night.

But still I spent a long time in the chair, just thanking God over and over. For Mike and what came of it and also for the cold turkey sandwiches turning out so well.

The world was really looking up.

19

The next morning, I was assigned cleanup duty. As if that wasn't bad enough, the place to be cleaned up was my room. I thought it was just perfect the way it was, but, of course, Mom had other ideas. My only comfort was that she leaned on the girls just as hard to clean *their* rooms.

It took me all morning. I kept wondering whether that little triumph with the cold turkey sandwiches was going to condemn me to making lunches forever.

But no. I had piled in the middle of the floor all the dirty clothes I found. As I was scooping them into a laundry bag, Mom appeared in the door.

"It could look better. Your shelves are messy. But it's good enough. What would you like for lunch?"

And I said, "A picnic."

So she packed me some stuff to take out to the park. I couldn't pull down e-mail because the computer was downloading some stuff Mom had looked up, but it didn't matter. I was going to let the gang alone awhile. I thought it would be best to just cool it and let the dust settle.

Besides, I hadn't visited the park by myself for awhile.

Sugar Creek County Park was a couple miles long and one-fourth to one-half mile wide. It took in only a small part of Sugar Creek, which went for miles and miles through farmland.

The park was another world. Lots of trees and brush muffled the sounds of traffic and sirens and barking dogs—all the noise that insists on reminding you that you live on a planet with billions of other people. Frogs, turtles, raccoons, and more insects than you can imagine called the park home. Very rarely, I'd spot a snake or a muskrat. When I walked along the trails, it felt as if I could be doing exactly this a hundred years ago.

Sometimes I'd leave the trail, especially on the swamp loop, and just sit on a log in the middle of the woods. For a while it would be only me alone. Then I'd start noticing insects—dragonflies, butterflies, beetles on the leaves. Flies. Ants. Lots of flies and ants. Then the birds would forget I was there and go about their business, sometimes pretty close.

I thought about doing all of those things this particular day and decided to do something different. I almost never went clear to the far end of the park. That's where I'd go this time.

I took off my bike helmet and hung it on the handlebars because I hate wearing it. Out in traffic or anywhere near traffic, it stays on. But today I would be riding two miles in granny gear—and nowhere near a paved road. I would be the only traffic.

I dropped my gears down to the lowest possible and pedaled back on the trail through the woods. I swung around the swamp loop just because I like it. The big turtle was not out today, but heaps of little turtles were crowded together along the top of a floating log, sunning. I stopped to count them. As I watched, one more turtle tried to climb up on the log. With a gentle swish, the log rolled over. The whole slew of turtles slid into the water, and I'll bet the ones that were snoozing woke up mighty surprised. When I left, a few were climbing clumsily back on the log.

The swamp loop crossed a little log bridge and rejoined the main trail. I helloed a man and woman who passed me, walking back toward the trailhead. And then I had gone about as far as I could go.

At this far end of the park, the woods opened up into a weedy meadow splashed with wildflowers and waist-high brush. Already, milkweed and clusters of thistle plants here and there across the meadow were spinning clumps of white silk. Summer couldn't be over this fast, could it?

Scratchy brown weeds tangled in my spokes and pedals, so I laid the bike down and walked out across the meadow. Now the scratchy brown weeds tangled in my shoelaces and stuck sharp little seeds in my socks.

If there were any deer around to see, they would come here to this meadow or along the brushy wood margin, where open grass met forest. A lonely, gnarled old oak tree squatted out in the middle of the meadow. Maybe if I just stood under that tree and watched and waited, I'd see one.

I hadn't gotten anywhere near the oak yet when a doe exploded out of the woods to the southeast. She bounded along at full speed, all four feet off the ground at once and her white tail flashing. Tiny once told me that whitetail deer signal each other with their tails that way.

What could spook her so badly?

She was a mama, because here came her baby, running full tilt also. The little guy was doing the best he could, but the weeds were taller than he was.

And then this huge spear of pure ice slashed down through me, chilling my heart and chest. I saw what was chasing the deer. They came barreling out onto the meadow close behind the fawn.

Wolves.

I didn't stop to think, and, believe me, I should have. I ran forward toward the fawn and the wolves, yelling and waving my arms.

The fawn was so scared he didn't pay much attention to me. He darted right past me, very close. He just kept running after mama as fast as he could. But the animals behind him faltered. They stopped and turned aside, snarling and snapping.

And they weren't wolves after all, although the leader might have had some wolf blood in him. He had to be over a hundred pounds; he was *big*. His blue eyes glinted. He had more than a little German shepherd or husky in him—probably both. He was grizzled gray like a shepherd, but German shepherds hold their tails down. Huskies curl their tails over their backs. His angled upward, half and half.

Two others, mixed breeds of some kind, might have been litter mates. They were gray, also. And the black chow-chow with them looked just plain nasty. His lips curled above his teeth. He wore a collar.

The smallest one wore a collar, too. *And I recognized him.*

I was no longer worried about Mrs. Monroe's Tuffy getting eaten by a wolf.

Tuffy *was* one of the wolves.

20

Long ago in a galaxy far away—that is, at my school in Seattle—every Friday was Safety Friday. We'd have an assembly in the afternoon, and an outsider would talk to us about safety. A firefighter would come in during Fire Prevention Month and teach us to drop and roll. A lifeguard would show slides of what not to do at the pool. That kind of thing.

One of those assemblies was about vicious dogs. An animal handler told us what to do if a dog challenged us. I could not remember a single solitary thing she'd said.

And right this moment, with five dogs snarling at me, I really, *really* wished I had paid better attention.

But Tuffy, little old Tuffy, wasn't a vicious dog, was he?

"Hey, Tuffy." I said the name again loudly. "*Tuffy!* We're friends, remember?"

Tuffy wasn't having any of it.

When Mrs. Monroe said her phone number was on his collar, I'd assumed she meant on a metal tag. No, it was written with a thick, black marking pen in huge numerals right on the nylon webbing of his collar, easy to read.

I made a quick mental note of the number.

It took me a moment to realize how stupid that was. Where was I going to get a phone?

I realized then why Tuffy had growled at me the day he tore his ear. He had just been out with his buddies, and he was still "wild."

The dogs were wild now.

I glanced toward the oak. It was too far. I could never outrun them that far. Then one of the dog handler's rules did come to mind: *Never run from a hostile dog.* Dogs are wired to chase things, the handler told us. If you run, they'll automatically chase you without even thinking about it, when maybe if you hadn't bolted, they wouldn't have.

There was nowhere else to go.

Oh, God, help me! Send someone! Do something!

Another rule came to mind. *Never stare at a hostile dog.* The dog takes it as a challenge. So I tried to keep a close eye on them without looking directly at any of them.

And dogs, I remembered then, like to attack from behind. *Don't let them get behind you.*

These dogs were hesitating for some reason. Maybe their training was getting in the way of attacking a human being. I bet they wouldn't have hesitated if I'd been a deer or a sheep. Or a toddler.

But then the lead dog moved in closer, snarling, and the two gray ones started circling to my left. The black chow began slinking around my right. I was guessing it was the chow who would go for my back or the backs of my legs.

I saw what was going to happen, but I didn't know how to stop it. Didn't know what to do.

Lord, help!

I couldn't outrun them. I couldn't outfight them. I couldn't climb anything. I couldn't even back up against something to protect the rear. If I had just gotten closer to that tree!

There was only one thing left to do. I was sure I would get bitten, but I'd have to chance it. I dropped forward, face down on the ground. I pulled my knees and elbows in under my belly. I knotted myself into as tight and smooth a wad as I could. With my legs under me and my elbows tucked in, I locked my fingers across the back of my neck, so that my arms protected my face and ears.

They could still chomp on me all they wanted, but they'd have to work at it, with nothing sticking out that fit easily into those horrible mouths. I could hear my own heart pounding. I waited, terrified, for that first ripping bite.

And waited . . .

Then I heard howling away off by the woods. Oh, no! These weren't the only dogs in the pack! Others were joining them!

The howling came closer.

But, no, it wasn't howling; it was yelling. People's voices yelling. Kids' voices yelling!

And I knew those voices!

I wanted to leap up and scream, "Run away! Run for your lives!" I should have done that, but I didn't. You know how people say they're petrified, when they mean they're scared? Stiff as stone? I really was petrified. I couldn't move. I just stayed in that tight curl while the world swirled and snarled somewhere out there.

The snarling and the yelling both got louder and louder. Then something grabbed my shoulder, and I was sure I was going to get eaten alive. The noise died down.

"Les?" Lynn's voice. "Les! It's OK. You're safe." Hands were pulling on me. Human hands. Not teeth.

"Les, did they get you?" Tiny's voice.

"No. You got here in time." I sat up and rocked back on my heels mostly because they were dragging me up. I felt weird. Dizzy.

"They're *dogs!*" Mike was turning inside out he was so excited. He still gripped a dead branch that was long enough to reach a star. "We got a good look at them. They're dogs! Did you see 'em good?"

"Yeah." I shuddered. "I even got their phone number."

It was over.

Not only did God send help when I asked, He sent the Sugar Creek Gang!

And then I started crying.

21

I certainly don't recommend getting attacked by wild dogs. In fact, I strongly recommend against it. But once in a very great while—a very, *very* great while—it pays off.

It paid off now when the gang sort of scooped me up out of that weedy meadow. I was still so shaky scared I had trouble keeping my bike on the path. We left the park and rode straight to the world's greatest ice cream stand by the museum. And the gang paid for my ice cream!

Even at the ice cream stand, sitting in a chair, I was shaking. My cone vibrated a little in my hand. "I don't get it, you guys. How did you show up there like that? And why? I thought you were all mad at each other."

"You see?" Bits flapped her hands. "I told you he doesn't read his e-mail."

"Where should we start?" Lynn was hard at work on a single dip of peanut-butter-chocolate. "It's a lot of different things that came together."

"I'll start with me." Bits had a double dip of marshmallow Neapolitan. "Night before last when we got back, Daddy could tell we'd been fighting. And when he asked about it, I kind of came apart. Really screamed and raved about how lousy all you guys were and how you were saying these terrible things about me. And when I finally stopped for breath, all he said was, 'I'm glad your friends love you enough to tell you the truth.'"

Tiny's eyebrows popped up. "He's smarter than I thought. He didn't yell back at you?"

Bits snorted. "If he had yelled at me, it would have been easier to stay mad. All he did was look real sad with those big brown eyes of his. Les, I apologize. I'm sorry."

Mike slurped the spoon from his vanilla hot fudge sundae. "I didn't dare do no yellin'. I'da got in trouble you wouldn't believe. But I was just as mad. So I sat on my bed that night and counted my money. I thought I was a dime short. And I was thinking, *Who stole my dime?* Then I thought, *Wait a minute, enchilada-head. Here you are accusing your own parents and brothers of stealing nothing. That's all a dime is. Nothing. And they all love you! What's the matter with you?* And I got thinking how maybe you were right, Bits. And you too, Les. I didn't like to believe you, but you were right."

Tiny chimed in. "So this morning, Mike came over to my place and said he wanted to apologize to you two, so we got on the e-mail and spread the word to meet at the park. It was easier than trying to find each other at home."

Mike nodded. "I already apologized to everyone else. I apologize to you, Les."

Lynn was nearly finished with her cone already. "I got to the picnic area after the others did because I came around the back way from O'Leary Avenue. And I saw these big gray dogs going over a stile into the park. I wondered if maybe those were the 'wolves.' Remember what Dr. Morgan said about feral dogs? When I got to the park I told the rest of them what I saw."

Bits pointed to Tiny. "And Daniel Boone here looks at some tracks on the ground and says, 'I bet that's Les's bike going back through the woods. Same kind of tires as ours.' So we followed your bike tracks and looked for the dogs at the same time."

Tiny grimaced. "Found 'em at the same time, too."

"Wow." I took another lick. That's all I could think of to say. So I said it again. "Wow."

"What do we do now?" Lynn asked.

"Call my dad and tell him," Bits suggested.

"Where's the nearest pay phone?" I asked. "I'm gonna call my dad, too."

Lynn pointed. "Museum lobby."

As soon as we were done nourishing the inner man, as Dad would put it, we headed up the big, wide museum steps. The phones were just inside the door in an alcove. Bits fished in her pocket for change.

Tiny handed her a couple quarters. "I'm going to go tell Dr. Morgan what we found. Or leave him a note if he's not there." He strode off across the shiny marble floor.

That was a good idea. I was thinking that if I washed out as a great chef, maybe Tiny and I could be great naturalists together.

While Bits jammed in the coins and punched her numbers, I wondered what I would say to Dad. "Hey, Dad, guess what. I almost got eaten alive." Nah. My folks would never let me leave the yard again. "You know those wolves? It's worse than wolves." Nah. Or maybe, "Oh, nothing much. Just the usual danger and mayhem. And how was *your* day?"

My attention snapped back to Bits. She had just said, "And they attacked Les!" A pause. "No, really! We saw him fall down on the ground, and we thought they ripped his throat out, but he was just protecting himself." Pause.

Just protecting myself?

"At the museum." Bits stared at the far wall a minute. "OK. We'll wait here." She hung up. "Daddy says he's coming over here. And you don't have to call your dad, Les. Daddy is going to call him and talk to him." She frowned. "Daddy sounded pretty upset."

"I don't blame him," said Lynn. "I think this is more serious than we realized. Like Tiny said, what if they went after a little child? I mean, Les is small enough. What if we'd waited for him at the picnic area and didn't go back there?"

I didn't want to think about it.

"Maybe your fathers will know what to do about the dogs." Mike polished off the last of his ice cream.

I nodded. "I'm glad they're both coming. I probably wasn't going to call mine anyway. I'm a dime short."

Mike reached into his pocket. "I got a dime here." He held it out to me. He looked sheepish. "I was wrong about somebody stealing from me. I found it in my bedcovers this morning."

22

It was 5:00 P.M. My mystery-novel-trained mind figured out what time it was from the clues. The clues were: (1) The museum chased everyone out and locked up. (2) They close at five.

So we sat in a line on the museum steps, like crows on a fence rail.

Someone in a white shirt and tie and black suit came out a side door. "You young people will have to move on. We don't allow loitering."

Bits replied, "We're waiting for our dads."

The man was going to say something else—probably chase us off—but Bits simply pointed toward the parking lot. Here came her father in full police uniform. Suddenly it was OK to loiter. The man said good-bye and went back inside.

My dad arrived right behind Sergeant Ware. They had plenty of parking slots to choose from—the lot was emptying quickly.

Sergeant Ware climbed the steps and sat down beside us. "So you got eaten alive, huh, Les?"

"I'm still too scared to make fun about it."

"I don't blame you. Good evening, Bill," he said to my dad.

"Evening, Jim." Dad looked at me. "Can you describe the dogs?"

I could. We all could. And we did. Then I told them about the phone number Mrs. Monroe marked on Tuffy's collar. I was surprised that I could remember it. The human brain is a weird thing.

The two men looked at each other.

Sergeant Ware started jotting notes rapidly. "Give me that number again."

I did.

He scribbled a minute and then asked, "Les, did Tuffy's collar have that number on it when you found him and took him back a couple days ago?"

"He wasn't wearing his collar then. First time I saw it was in the meadow this afternoon."

Both men nodded silently.

Dad asked, "The other dog with a collar—could you make out a name or read anything on the tags?"

"No, sir. I didn't want to get that close. In fact, I didn't want to get as close as I did."

Dad snickered, but he turned serious again instantly. "Jim, is the law what I think it is?"

Sergeant Ware nodded.

"Think we can do anything tonight yet?"

The officer nodded again as he stood up.

"Do what?" Bits looked from face to face. Her voice was getting that edge to it again.

"We'll start with Tuffy, then track down the other dogs and their owners. All five."

"But *then* what? Catch them?"

"If we can. Shoot them if we can't."

"Shoot *Tuffy*?"

"Kids, it's not nice, I know." Sergeant Ware included us all as he spoke. "But we have a solid identification, and when those dogs turned on Les they proved how dangerous they are. We're wrong if we don't do something. According to the law, this situation allows us to kill them. And as a public safety officer, I'm required to do something about the problem."

Bits looked furious. "I'm sorry I called you!"

"Are you sorry for all the animals they hurt and kill? Or for the little kid who's bound to get in their way one of these days?" He pulled the cell phone on his belt and punched in some numbers. He waited a few seconds and punched in some more—extension numbers, probably.

He held it to his ear. "Hi, Grace. No, I'm working a little late. Need a phone check." From his notebook he read off the number I had given him.

It didn't take Grace, whoever Grace was, long to find out who belonged to the number. Sergeant Ware repeated it. "M-O-N-R-O-E. Got it. Thanks, Grace." He clapped the phone shut and told Bits, "Grace says hi." So Grace and Bits knew each other.

I felt as sad as you can get. I could tell by the way they drooped that Tiny and Mike and Bits felt the same way. We started down the long, long bank of steps toward the parking lot.

"Wait. Where's Lynn?" I turned to look.

She was still sitting on the steps, silent, leaning forward with her face buried in her hands.

What could you do? Bits knew. She jogged right back up the steps, sat down beside Lynn, and wrapped her arms around her. Lynn sort of melted over against her, and they just sat like that, comforting each other. I could see Bits was crying, too.

Sergeant Ware said quietly, "Bill, we'd better get these kids home first. It's suppertime."

Dad nodded.

But Tiny said, "No. Please, Mr. Walker—Sergeant Ware. We been up against this wolf business since the beginning—all of us—since the first chewed-up rabbit got brought in with a leg missing. We came up against them today again. We want to see it through."

"Yes, but—" Dad started.

"I know. Kids ain't s'posed to be exposed to death and violence. I'm saying, sir, we already been exposed to it since the beginning of this. We already know what they do, and we understand what has to be done yet. Please let us stay with you."

The sergeant looked at Mike.

Mike nodded. "I want to go. Please."

I nodded, too.

Dad climbed the steps and crouched down in front of Lynn and Bits. He loaned them his handkerchief. All three of them muttered awhile. The girls nodded, and then nodded again.

When Dad stood up and turned, the girls stood up, too, and strode down the steps with him. You could see they'd been crying, but they looked just as determined and strong as everyone else. They were going to see it through, too.

We were a pretty gloomy bunch as we crawled into Dad's car and the sergeant's pickup. We all knew that before this mess got any better, it was going to get a whole lot worse.

23

Tuffy was curled up asleep on his porch when our two vehicles pulled into Mrs. Monroe's driveway. He jumped up and barked dutifully. Mrs. Monroe opened her front door as we were getting out.

She stepped down off the porch and smiled. "I'm having chicken for dinner. I'm sorry I didn't fix enough for guests."

Sergeant Ware grimaced. I suppose he thought it was a smile. "Mrs. Monroe, is this your telephone number?" He showed her a notebook page.

She craned her head a bit. "Yes, it is."

Dad had let Tuffy sniff his hand, and now he was twisting Tuffy's collar around so that all could see the number on it. He didn't say anything. No one had to.

Mrs. Monroe looked at Dad, at the sergeant in his police officer's uniform, at us. "What's going on here?"

"Your little dog, Tuffy, was out with a pack of feral dogs this afternoon. They were chasing a deer when Les here interfered. They turned on him."

"You're mistaken. Tuffy doesn't do that." She listened to the silence a moment and apparently couldn't stand it. She raised her voice a couple notches. "I assure you, Tuffy wouldn't do that! He knows Les." She stared at the girls, so I looked at them, too.

They were still all puffy eyed and wet nosed.

Dad stepped forward. "Mrs. Monroe, we haven't met, but I've heard very good things about you. I'm Les's father, Bill Walker." He extended his hand.

She took it cautiously, distrustfully. "I'm surprised Les thought Tuffy would do such a thing."

Dad crossed his arms. He looked very large. "Mrs. Monroe, dogs do what dogs do. I suspect you know that. When they get going in groups —in packs—they'll chase, given the chance. Chase and kill."

"Maybe huge, dangerous dogs. Certainly not my little Tuffy!"

Sergeant Ware said, "All dogs. It's their nature. They're fine when they're in the home, in a family situation. But running loose, they revert to wild ways. It's just their nature to do that."

Mrs. Monroe glared at me. "You got that phone number when you brought Tuffy home that day! Les, how could you!"

"No, ma'am. He wasn't wearing a collar then, remember?"

Then she stared angrily at Dad. "You're try-ing to pin something on my little dog! You need a scapegoat and so—"

And Dad exploded. "Those dogs attacked

my son!" He roared so ferociously that she stepped back a step.

She looked stunned for a long moment. Her voice dropped to almost a whisper. "Do I have to put Tuffy down?"

Lynn pressed her hand over her mouth, but she kept her cool.

Sergeant Ware said quietly, "The attack took place in Sugar Creek County Park. That is within my jurisdiction. I'm empowered to cite you and impound the dog, if necessary. I don't want it to be necessary. Can you keep Tuffy under physical control at all times? A tie rope? A fence?"

"But he's too used to roaming. It would be cruel to confine him!"

Tiny spoke up. "Miz Monroe, you ain't seen the rabbits and deer and sheep and turkeys—all the animals they hurt for the fun of it. Tying Tuffy up won't be half as cruel as what they're doing to other things."

She looked at Dad and Sergeant Ware. Then she said quietly, "I'll build a fence. I'll keep him tied until then."

Mike said, "Ma'am? My brothers and I, we've built fences before. You get the stuff—the wire and stuff—and the gang here, we'll help you build it. For free. Won't cost you much that way."

All of us Creekers jumped on that one, eagerly offering our services.

Bits's dad was nodding now and smiling. "Bill and I can lend a hand, too. Now we need your help. We have to contact the owners of the other dogs . . ."

"I know every family in this township and just about all their dogs. Describe them."

An hour later, the job was done. One of the owners wasn't nearly as nice as Mrs. Monroe. He wasn't going to cooperate the way she did until Sergeant Ware explained the county's shoot-on-sight law. Also, Dad threatened to take him to court. Dad used the words *initiate a civil action*, and that's why I don't plan to be a lawyer when I grow up. They don't speak English. But his threat worked. The man decided to keep his black chow fenced in.

That night when I opened up my window and sat down in my chair, I had plenty to be thankful to the Lord about. Sometimes when I would say thank You in a prayer, the only thing I'd thank Him for was for making me His child through Jesus. But this time, look at all He did for me—for all of us! I got saved from the dogs. We solved the wolf problem. The gang had healed.

And there was old Mike, the penny pincher. He was the first one to offer to help Mrs. Monroe. For *free*. It looked to me like God really did a work on him.

And I was finally on my way to becoming a great chef.